Rebecca Parkinson

Riches in
Romania

© Day One Publications 2012

First printed 2012

ISBN 978-1846253607

All Scripture quotations are from the **New International Version** 1984
Copyright © 1973, 1978, 1984

Published by Day One Publications
Ryelands Road, Leominster, HR6 8NZ

TEL 01568 613 740 FAX 01568 611 473

email—sales@dayone.co.uk

UK web site—www.dayone.co.uk

USA web site—www.dayonebookstore.com

Printed by Orchard Press Cheltenham Ltd

Dedication

With love for our special Romanian friends
... you taught us so much.

1 Ivonia

*I*vonia gently lifted the coarse, woollen blanket and
wriggled carefully down between her sleeping sisters
to the end of the bed. She glanced at them momentarily.
Laura was older than her by 18 months; she looked so
pretty and peaceful, her light brown hair spread out on the
pillow like a spiky crown. On her other side lay Ana, the
baby of the family. Not that she actually was a baby any
longer, she had grown up so quickly recently and it would
soon be her third birthday! Ivonia smiled as Ana stuck
her thumb in her mouth, turned over and began to suck
noisily.

Quietly, she tiptoed across the threadbare carpet,
wrapping her dad's coat round her shoulders before
opening the front door. A blast of icy air slapped her face
and she quickly pulled up the furry collar to cover her
cheeks. It was springtime but the weather was still cold
and a wise old man in the village had predicted a spring
snowfall.

She hurried across the courtyard to a small shed that
stood alone a short distance from the house and clicked
open the door. A shiver ran through her body, but she
smiled.

"At least the cold weather means it's not so smelly in
here!" she whispered to herself.

The toilet was so much better since Papa had decorated it. The half-used tin of paint, given to them by a kindly neighbour, had whitewashed all the wood and resulted in a cleaner, fresher feel.

She stretched up to smell the dangling bag of lavender left by an Australian visitor to the village. The pleasant smell had long since disappeared but it still looked pretty and she knew it would not be thrown away.

Ivonia shuddered as a cold draught blew through the shed, disturbing her thoughts and making her hurry even more. She skipped back across the courtyard and stopped by the deep well to wash her hands in a bucket of water that her papa had drawn up the previous evening. The neighbourhood dogs were already beginning to stir and the birds twittered cheerfully in the trees as if announcing the arrival of dawn. She rested for a moment on the rickety wooden bench beside the gate and happily ran a finger over the frozen gatepost, the warmth of her hands making fingerprints in the ice. Then, with one bound, she leapt up onto the bench and peered over the fence surrounding the house to gaze at the nearby fields and hills which were shimmering as the early morning sun reflected off the frost.

"My beautiful Romania," she sighed. "There can be nowhere else in the world like this place."

She turned and faced the house, lovingly built by her parents when they were first married. There was nothing she loved more than to sit round the stove in the evening, listening as Papa reminisced about its building.

"Your mother built non-stop for three years," he would say, leaning back in his chair with a twinkle in his eye.

CHAPTER ONE

"The only time she stopped was to give birth to the three of you ..." He would turn and nod at Laura, Stefan and Ivonia before he continued.

"Best thing I ever did, marrying your mama! Needed some help with the building ... I married her for her muscles. Got muscles firmer than any man!"

He would playfully squeeze Mama's upper arms and look at her in a way that somehow conveyed clearly that he married for love not muscle!

The family had moved into the house when Ivonia was three months old. The next four years had seen the birth of two boys, Petru and Adi, and then three years later Ana had arrived.

The house was hardly big enough for eight people, especially as they grew older, but it was homely and Ivonia vowed that she would never move away. It contained only three rooms. The sparsely furnished parlour was rarely used, except for special occasions like birthdays or Christmas. The kitchen housed the large brick stove where Mama made her delicious bread. The living room was used for every other activity! A tall dresser took up the majority of one wall. Most of the doors had fallen off and been used as fire-wood long ago and the shelves displayed the family's meagre possessions. A large stone heater, characteristic of all Romanian homes, stretched from floor to ceiling in one corner. It was roughly the size of a wardrobe and was covered in ornate brown polished tiles with a small metal door in its base, through which wood would be added. This was the only source of heat for the house and there was always a race to be the first to sit beside it when freezing feet needed warming in the winter!

Other than a fold-away table and three brown settees, there was no other furniture in the room. Each evening the settees would be folded down into beds and bedding dragged from the top of the dresser, allowing all the family to snuggle down to sleep at the same time. These were always moments of great hilarity and giggling, until Mama or Papa ordered 'silence.' Then they would all sleep till dawn-break, three boys in one bed, three girls in another, and Mama and Papa in the third. Mama always said that God knew they needed equal numbers of boys and girls in their family so they could all fit in a bed!

*   *   *

The sound of laughter floating out into the cold air from the open window interrupted Ivonia's thoughts and sent her scurrying indoors. The boys were having their daily pillow fight, Ana was running round and round in circles with her trousers on her head and Laura was pulling out the foldaway table ready for breakfast.

Dodging to avoid the boys, Ivonia moved to the kitchen where Mama looked up from the stove and smiled.

"You were up early!" she laughed. "I wonder why?"

"I couldn't sleep," Ivonia whispered in a dreamy voice. "One more day…"

She raised her eyebrows and sighed, "… and then they'll come!"

2 Jenny

On an ordinary morning Jenny would lie in bed for as long as possible with the duvet pulled up to her chin whilst she contemplated getting up. Today she lay still for only a moment, her eyes scanning round her newly decorated room. She loved the lilac wallpaper, the furry rug, the matching furniture and the vast array of toys and books piled on her shelves. A tingle of excitement ran through her body as she shot out of bed.

"Wakey, wakey! Rise and shine! The morning's fine! Don't turn over, turn out!!" she bellowed at the top of her voice, repeating a rhyme her Granddad had taught her.

She heard creaking movements as her parents moved about getting dressed and a grunt echoed from her brother's room. She sprinted across the landing, opened his door and dived on top of David, landing directly on his stomach.

"Ow! Get off me stupid!" her brother yelled, shoving her off the bed.

"Don't shove me, you big baby," Jenny shouted back, rubbing her injured knee.

"Then don't land your fat body on my stomach!"

"I'm not fat ... that's you ..."

"YOU TWO STOP IT!" Dad's voice boomed angrily across the landing. "Get up both of you and finish packing. We need to be at the airport in three hours!

For once both children obeyed.

Back in her room Jenny added a few final necessities to her case and padlocked it shut. She smiled. Her friends would all be getting ready for school now, but not her! In just a few hours' time she would be boarding a plane to Milan and then another to fly them into Bucharest, the capital of Romania.

It would be lovely to fly again. There had been a time when Jenny and her family were always jetting around the world from one exotic location to another, much to the envy of all her friends. Now everything had changed!

What a difference two years could make. Jenny sat down on the edge of the bed, sighing as she remembered the dreadful night when, unable to sleep, she had wandered downstairs and overheard her parents rowing in the kitchen. The memory of those words still felt painful, even now ...

"We can't go on like this," Mum had shouted. "You're always at work! We never see you and when you are here you're in such a bad mood that we all wish you hadn't bothered to come home anyway!"

"Then maybe I won't come home anymore," Dad had retaliated. "Nag, nag, nag! That's all you ever do!"

"It might be better without you!" Mum began to cry.

Jenny didn't wait to hear any more. She fled upstairs and fell asleep sobbing into her pillow.

During the weeks that followed the house was always full of arguing and shouting, except when visitors came round and everyone pretended things were okay! Then something happened.

The family had attended church for as long as Jenny could remember, but this particular Sunday was different. Jenny had spent the morning in Sunday school. Once the service had ended, she returned to the main church to find her dad sitting on the front row with the minister's arm around his shoulder. Mum was sitting in her usual seat but a friend was next to her, holding her hand, and it was obvious she had been crying.

A feeling of complete horror filled Jenny, and without thinking, she burst into tears screeching, "Please Mum, please, please don't split up!"

There had been an awkward silence before Mum pulled her gently on to her knee, speaking loudly enough for the silenced room to hear.

"Don't worry, darling. Your dad and I aren't splitting up. It's just that God has spoken to us this morning and things need to change."

Ever since that day Jenny had wanted to ask how God had spoken, or if anyone else had heard him, or if his voice was loud or quiet or if he had an accent! For some reason she had never dared to ask, but she knew that from that moment on things certainly did change.

Her dad returned from work the next day having 'given in his notice'—which apparently meant he wasn't going to work at the same place anymore. After two weeks Mum began to work for a few hours a day in the local supermarket and Dad got a job with a local charity that helped set up farming projects among poor people in different areas of the world.

The drop in Dad's wages meant the children's lifestyle would never be the same again. They no longer had expensive holidays, trips to the theatre or other treats that they had become so accustomed to; but the house was less 'stressy' and much happier.

The changes didn't seem to affect David. All he ever wanted to do was roll around in the mud playing football, and you could do that for free! Jenny however had struggled. Of course she was glad her family was happy again, but she missed the envious looks of her friends when she appeared in the latest fashions and talked about outings that the others could only dream of.

"Breakfast's ready you two!"

Mum's shout from downstairs interrupted her thoughts.

Jenny jumped up. At least they were off on an adventure now! Dad had returned from work a week ago and announced that the charity was sending him to help set up a potato farm in a small village in Romania and they wanted him to take his family along with him! It had been rather a rush to organise everything but they were almost ready to go.

"Two weeks off school!" Jenny sang as she bounded downstairs.

She sat at the table trying to push away the horrible feelings that the thought of school brought to her mind. NO! She would not think about it. She gobbled her breakfast down quickly.

"Jenny love, do you want to ring any of your friends to say goodbye before we go?"

Jenny looked up to see Mum giving her the knowing look that always made Jenny cringe.

"Not Amy or anyone?"

Jenny sprang up.

"NO! I DO NOT!" she snapped. "I don't even want to hear her name!"

She stormed out of the room leaving Mum staring after her, a concerned expression on her face.

Jenny threw herself down on her bed.

"Why?" she seethed through gritted teeth. Why did Amy always spring into her thoughts at the most inconvenient moments?

AMY!! Her ex-best friend! Jenny shook her head. At least she had two weeks away from her and there was no way that she was going to spoil this holiday!

3 Waiting!

"**I**vonia!" Mama's voice called from the courtyard. She straightened her back and for a moment stopped scrubbing at Papa's trousers in the large tin bath.

"Ivonia, why don't you come inside and have a drink? Ivan and Helena won't be here for at least an hour."

"But Mama, they may be early!" Ivonia's voice carried on the wind from the other side of the fence.

"And if you stand in the middle of that muddy road much longer you'll have to get changed and meet your visitors in your scruffs!"

Mama knew that would do the trick; Ivonia fled inside checking herself up and down for any traces of mud!

Mama smiled. Ivonia usually took so little interest in her appearance and was often filthy from head to toe after working outside on their land. She was only 10 years old but today she looked like a young lady. Her long brown hair was tied back in a ponytail and the pale pink headscarf covering most of her hair was neatly knotted under her hairline. Last month's visit from the charity van had produced a particularly good selection of clothes for Ivonia's age group and the light green jumper not only went well with the long brown skirt but also highlighted the colour of her eyes.

Mama had such a lot to do today but she put down her washing in a determined manner. It was rare to have a few spare minutes to spend time with just one of the children, and Ivonia looked so grown up that Mama was suddenly reminded that childhood is such a short time and moments like these needed to be grasped.

Cuddled on the settee with a warm drink, Ivonia felt the preciousness of the moment too. Papa had gone to town and taken Ana with him. The other children were in school. Ivonia had been allowed to stay at home today to meet the visitors.

"Mama," she raised her eyes to her mother, who could read a mixture of excitement and fear in them. "Mama, do you think she'll like me?"

Mama gently ran her finger around Ivonia's upturned face and spoke quietly.

"Ivonia, I have never met anyone who does not like you. You are lovely on the outside but more importantly you are good and kind, loving and honest on the inside. Papa and I are so proud of you." She laughed and spoke in a silly accent. "The English girl is crazy if she doesn't love you!"

A loud knock on the door made them jump. Ivan's face appeared at the window, his wife Helena beside him.

Ivonia leapt up.

"Mama, I said they'd be early. Sorry Ivan!"

Ivan smiled, his eyes twinkling brightly.

"We are very early," he said. "We thought we might call in and get an ice-cream in town en-route, if Ivonia doesn't mind?"

Everyone laughed at the look on Ivonia's face—there was no doubt about her answer!

Sitting in the backseat of the car, Ivonia held on tightly as Ivan swerved from side to side avoiding the potholes. The road passing through the centre of the village was little more than a wide, well pressed-down mud path running at right-angles off the main road to the nearby town. The track sloped steeply upwards for approximately half a kilometre before opening out onto a large area of open farmland at the top. Small streets joined the road at intervals, along which were dotted small, wooden houses with brightly coloured fences surrounding them. Separating the houses were small strips of land which the villagers owned and cultivated to provide food. There were people working in the fields now and Ivonia waved grandly as Ivan pipped his horn to attract the workers' attention.

Ivonia had been in cars before, but not often. The family was certainly not rich enough to own a car and in any case neither of her parents could drive. There were lots of cars in Romania, almost all box-shaped Ladas, but in the villages it was still more common to use a horse and cart. Ivonia's parents didn't own one of those either but neighbours shared their possessions and Papa could always borrow one if he needed to.

Ivan turned on to the main concreted road and the journey became more comfortable until a horse and cart pulled out from a side road straight in front of them, causing him to slam on his brakes. Ivan simply pipped the horn and laughed. Ivonia often thought that was the best thing about Ivan: he was always laughing. Even when things happened that made other people mad, his eyes would still twinkle as if his heart were full of joy and he didn't have a care in the world.

Helena turned round and offered Ivonia a sweet.

"Shall we practise some English?" she asked. "Your last chance to practise before you meet the English girl!"

Ivonia nodded. She had been learning English with Helena for a year now. Helena taught part-time in the village school and had noticed that Ivonia seemed to have a natural ability to pick up languages. She had approached Mama and Papa to see if they would agree to Ivonia having extra lessons with her, in the hope that as she improved she could help the younger children in school.

Tuesday and Wednesday nights had become the highlights of Ivonia's week. School finished at two o'clock and she would return home to complete her chores. At four thirty she would walk down the road to Ivan and Helena's home for a one-hour lesson, after which they would eat tea together.

As much as Ivonia enjoyed the lessons it was tea time that she loved the most. The house wasn't large but it was one of the more modern buildings in the village. It had the same brown tiled heater as every other home but somehow it always felt warmer and brighter. Ivan and Helena would talk of when they first met and their dreams for the future. Helena would describe her childhood in the south of Romania and her studies in England, where her mother's family still lived. Ivan said little of his family or his past but somehow Ivonia got the impression that it was sad and so she never asked any questions.

Ivan pulled up outside a small shop with tables and chairs dotted at random on the pavement in front of it. He glanced at his watch.

"Loads of time," he announced. "Let's sit at the tables and eat!"

A tingle ran through Ivonia's body. She had never been to a café before and felt rather nervous as she read down the menu, glancing at Helena for some advice.

"Ivan will order," Helena reassured her. "You don't have to make any decisions. All you have to do is eat!"

Ivonia smiled gratefully.

"That bit will be easy," she said.

4 Broken friendship

Jenny settled back into her window seat and gazed along the length of the plane's wings. She had been looking forward to this moment when she would take to the air and fly away from England, leaving all her troubles behind her.

The engines fired and the plane gathered momentum, forcing the passengers back into their seats. The wing fins bent downwards and they were off, slicing through the air, houses shrinking to tiny dots until only a muddled mass of green and brown lay beneath them.

David sucked noisily on his hard-boiled sweet. For once Jenny didn't frown but opened and shut her own mouth, wiggling her jaw, trying desperately to release the pressure in her ears so they would pop.

It seemed like only moments passed before they saw the sea stretching out below them and the stewards appeared ready to serve the in-flight meals.

"Yeeesss!" shouted David, punching the air in victory. "At last! I'm starving." He opened his box and peered inside, raising his head with a look of disappointment!

"A sandwich?!" he demanded, lifting the top off his rather flattened bread roll.

"Yuk!! Cheese and gherkin!"

He fished the soggy gherkin out and dangled it in front of Mum.

"Why do they ruin good food with stuff like this?" he grumbled. "No-one on earth likes these!"

Jenny turned to look out of the window. It wasn't fair! Even a stupid, boxed up revolting meal seemed determined to remind her of the one person she knew who actually did like gherkins ... Amy!

Oh why did she have to feel so bad? For a moment she allowed herself to think.

Amy had arrived at school two months previously. She had been popular from the moment she entered the classroom, but, for some reason, she seemed to particularly want to be Jenny's friend. At first Jenny had been flattered and the two of them had become inseparable. It was a visit to Amy's house that had changed everything and now nothing would ever be the same again.

Jenny had known that Amy's dad had died when Amy was just four years old and that her mum didn't have a job. She assumed that Amy would live in a tiny house with a pokey garden and had taken great delight in showing her around their large four-bedroom detached home, quite sure that she would be extremely impressed.

The following week Amy's mum had picked Jenny up from school for a return visit, and after a short journey, pulled into the long driveway of a massive house surrounded by large gardens on every side.

Amy looked at Jenny, her eyes gleaming.

"Well?" she asked. "Do you like it? Won't we have fun playing here?"

"I ... i ... i ... is it yours?" Jenny spluttered, hardly able to form her words.

"Yes," Amy replied with a twinkle in her eyes. "I couldn't wait to show you. It was my grandparents' house but they left it to us when they died. Mum keeps talking about selling it but somehow neither of us want to leave! Come on! I'll show you round."

Moving from room to room, as Amy completed the grand tour, Jenny remained speechless. Eventually Amy stopped outside an upstairs door.

"Now," she announced. "I've saved this room until last. This is my room!"

She threw open the door and ushered Jenny inside. The room was at least three times the size of Jenny's bedroom. Three walls were lilac with tiny silver stars on them; the fourth wall was cream with a huge, beautiful mural of dolphins painted on it. Jenny felt she almost sank into the deep carpet. The pictures on the walls, the curtains, the toys, the games, even the rugs seemed to shout out to Jenny ...

"... Amy is richer than you are! You'll never have anything like this!"

Amy's eyes clouded over.

"What's the matter Jenny?" she whispered. "Don't you like it?"

Jenny swallowed. "Yes," she replied curtly. "It's very nice."

There was silence and Amy suggested they went into the garden. Jenny hardly noticed Amy talking more quickly than usual about David, Jenny's brother ... her own Dad ... her grandparents ... money. She had no idea what else!

"Oi Sis!!" David elbowed her. "You not eating this roll? It's just your poor starving brother needs it, gherkin or no gherkin!"

Jenny shrugged her shoulders. She didn't feel hungry.

"You have it," she muttered, turning back to gaze out at the blue sky stretching endlessly before her. She didn't want to continue thinking, but somehow she couldn't stop herself.

Jenny had said nothing as Amy showed her the gardens, each with a different function.

"This is the area where Grandma and Granddad used to hold barbeques in the summer. Mum says we can do that later in the year," Amy continued with slightly less enthusiasm.

"This is what we call the terraced garden because of all the different levels. That path's brilliant for chasing round and you can play the best games of hide and seek in the bushes ... and this is the play garden!"

Amy opened a gate to reveal what Jenny could only describe as a park complete with swing, slide, seesaw, playhouse, sandpit and a shed full of outdoor toys.

Jenny willed herself to speak but somehow no words came out.

"What's wrong Jenny?" Amy looked upset. "I thought you'd love everything. Are you not very well?"

"No," Jenny replied sharply. "I feel ill."

"Oh no!" said Amy, obviously concerned. "Let's get you inside then and tell Mum."

The girls walked back towards the house passing a large barn-like building. Amy squeezed Jenny's arm.

22

"I know you're not feeling very well," she whispered sympathetically. "But this might cheer you up. Mum's going to put a swimming pool in there later in the year. We'll be able to swim all summer!"

It wasn't often that Jenny lost her temper and even now as she sat in the plane, she felt her cheeks beginning to burn red with embarrassment as she thought about what had happened next.

She turned to Amy, angry jealousy firing up inside her.

"Who do you think you are, you little show-off?" she blurted out. "Making me think you were so poor and all alone since your dad died. Bringing me here to your house so you can gloat about all the things you've got. You're selfish Amy. Nothing but a spoilt little rich girl. You're not a real friend!"

She had regretted the words as soon as they were out; but words once they are spoken can never be taken back again.

Amy had burst into tears, and despite her mum's best efforts to sort things out, Jenny had been driven home early.

At school the next day Amy had tried to speak to her but Jenny was far too ashamed and just walked away. To make matters worse, Amy had told Sarah, the class gossip, about what happened and soon everyone in the school seemed to be talking behind Jenny's back. Amy tried to explain that she wouldn't have told Sarah if she had realised that she had such a big mouth, but it was too late. The damage was done and Jenny and Amy hadn't spoken since. Two weeks had passed and Jenny had become more and more unhappy but somehow couldn't find the courage

to say sorry, knowing that words could never be 'unsaid'
and that Amy could surely never forgive her.

Jenny blinked back her tears. How she regretted
that outburst. It wasn't as if she was usually a horrible
girl. She had always been popular, usually kind, usually
generous but just one angry, jealous outburst had ruined
the best friendship she had ever had.

"Can all passengers please fasten their seat belts?
We are shortly to land in Milan.
The temperature is ..."

Jenny fastened her belt and prepared to land. She had
two weeks away from school. How she hoped that time and
distance would somehow make things better.

5 The Welcome

The earliness of the hour and the dampness of the weather did nothing to enhance the appearance of Bucharest railway station. Jenny peered at the dark gloomy building through the car window with sleepy, bleary eyes. The flight from Milan to Bucharest had gone smoothly and the family had been met, as arranged, by a Romanian charity worker called Florin and taken to his home. It had been midnight when they had flopped, fully clothed into bed only to be woken at 5 a.m. by a loud knocking on the door. They had climbed, still dazed, into the car and been driven at speed through the city until Florin screeched the car to a stop and sprinted into the station to buy tickets.

The city hadn't yet surfaced from sleep and Jenny gazed out at the billboards at the sides of the roads, surprised to recognise so many well-known adverts. Famous English footballers smiled at them enticing them to buy expensive sportswear; mobile phone companies heralded the greatness of their brand with the same pictures as seen in England but with Romanian captions; Coca-Cola lived up to its fame as the drink sold throughout the world!

"That advert certainly works," muttered David. "I'm parched!"

He was still complaining when Florin returned with the tickets announcing that they had three-quarters of an hour before the train left.

"Time for a drink then?" questioned David. "Otherwise I may die!"

Mum frowned at him as they climbed out of the car and began to unload the cases.

"There may not be anywhere to get a drink David," she said firmly. "I've got some water in my bag."

"Water!" David protested. "What about breakfast?"

"You English?" a small, heavily accented voice spoke beside them. Everyone turned to see a child, possibly eight or nine years of age, gazing up at them with deep, pleading eyes.

"I help you?" he continued. "I carry bag?"

Suddenly, as if by magic, a crowd of almost identical, scruffily dressed children appeared all asking the same questions, except those with a lesser grasp of English who quietly mumbled, "English, English...Coca cola...!" over and over again.

Jenny clutched her Dad's hand as Florin shooed the children away with a flurry of Romanian. He noticed Jenny's questioning eyes and answered in broken English.

"In Bucharest there are many children who live on streets. Some have no home. Some have home but not money. We call them 'street children.' To live they do jobs like carry the suitcase ... or they beg or steal."

"But where do they sleep and why didn't we give them any money?" asked Jenny, watching a tiny girl sitting on a nearby bench whose hair was tangled and whose clothes were old and torn.

"There are so many," replied Florin holding up his hands and shaking his head. "Who you give to? Give to one and crowd appear. They sleep on the bench, in parks, in doorways. My friends at other side of city make meal for street children once a week!"

The conversation was cut short by David's loud, "Yeess!!" as they entered the station.

The brightly lit red and yellow 'MacDonald's' sign stood out in sharp contrast to the dreariness surrounding it. Dad laughed and without further comment everyone marched forward, and soon they were all enjoying breakfast!

Jenny nudged her mum.

"Have I time to go to the loo before the train leaves?" she asked, licking the last grains of salt from her lips.

"Fifteen minutes before leaving," Florin replied, having overheard the question. "And your, how is it you say?... 'loo' is down there."

He pointed to some stone steps and Mum took Jenny by the hand and led her towards them.

Standing at the top of the steps they exchanged concerned glances. A dim bare light bulb dangled from the ceiling at the bottom of the steps. It swung gently to and fro sending ghostly shadows up and down the walls, making Jenny shudder. Hunched at a small metal table at the base of the steps sat a large woman noisily jingling coins up and down methodically in her closed hands. She saw them and beckoned, just as Florin tapped Mum on the shoulder making her jump.

"Sorry," he spoke guiltily. "I forget you need money here. You pay lady this ..." he pushed a coin into Mum's hand. "... and she give you toilet paper. You need more paper ... you pay more money ..."

He thrust a few more coins at her.

Mum thanked him and tentatively started down the steps. Jenny's heart pounded as she clung to Mum's hand but suddenly Mum turned decisively and to Jenny's relief announced that the need for the toilet had worn off and she would go later. Jenny nodded her head in full agreement!

The eight hour train journey from Bucharest passed more quickly than expected. The children played games, listened to their iPods, slept and ate the copious amounts of food Mum had packed—even David seemed satisfied. Dad produced his Romanian phrase book and practiced on any passers-by, causing much amusement and resulting in many interested visitors to their carriage.

"Buna dimineata," one person after another uttered, breaking out into hysterical giggles as each member of the family in turn attempted to repeat the 'Good morning' greeting.

It was a strange journey. The small part of Bucharest they had seen that morning had not appeared significantly different to any UK city but, as they travelled up through the countryside towards the Ukraine border, the scenery changed dramatically. Small villages dotted the beautiful landscape, appearing picturesque from a distance but on closer inspection telling a different story. Some houses stood out like beacons, their wooden walls well painted, their gardens well cared for; others were little more than rickety wooden shacks with sheets of corrugated metal flimsily attached as a covering. Clothes were hanging pegged out in most gardens and Jenny wondered why anyone would hang out dirty clothes on a line to dry.

There was one village in particular that caught Jenny's eye. She didn't really know why two houses, out of all the hundreds they had seen, should stand out; perhaps, she thought, it was the normality of the scene.

Two ladies stood, each in their own garden, talking and laughing over the fence. In each garden young children were playing and as the train slowed, one child ran to watch it, tripping heavily over a stone. His mother sprang towards him, gathered him in her arms and immediately the boy stopped crying and everyone turned to wave at the train, delighted mischief on the children's faces! Jenny waved back, wondering how those families could smile when their tiny houses looked as if a gentle wind might blow them away. Her eyes rested again on the now comforted child, his arms and legs still wrapped firmly around his mother. He was fiddling with the knot at the back of her head scarf but suddenly he had had enough; he leaned back, planted a huge kiss on his mum's nose and jumped down to join his playmates. Both ladies laughed and for a moment Jenny saw, in that mother's eyes, the same look of love and happiness that she'd seen in her own parent's eyes when either she or David had done something to make them particularly proud.

Jenny had dozed off when the guard appeared in the carriage doorway gesturing that they were nearing their destination. Both children dashed to the window hoping for the first glimpse of their welcoming party. They had been told by Florin that a man called Ivan would be waiting to transport them to their accommodation and to bring Dad up-to-date with the farming project.

The train stopped. The guard opened the door, helped them down the steps, and motioned them onto a wide strip of concrete. Mum glanced anxiously up and down, wondering if they really were going to have to climb over the bare rail-tracks in order to reach the platform fifty metres away. There was a moment of uncertainty as the guard shut the doors, the train began to move and they were left alone in an unknown place. Jenny glanced down, suddenly aware that both she and David had taken hold of their parent's hands, giving them at least some sense of security. And then, as the train moved away, a man appeared at their side and suddenly all anxiety was taken away as he held out his hand, welcoming them with twinkling eyes.

"Hello! I am Ivan."

His wife stood beside him, smiling and greeting them in perfect English, and a young girl mouthed, "Hello," but was so stricken by shyness that she could say nothing else!

"This is Ivonia," Ivan spoke gently, looking at Jenny as he did so. "She is ten, the age that you are. She has been so looking forward to meeting you."

6 Nothing at all

The car journey back to Ivonia's village was, in Dad's words, 'an experience'; in Mum's 'a nightmare'; in Jenny's 'uncomfortable'; and in David's words 'awesome!'

Ivan had not seemed to consider that fitting seven people and their luggage into a small car may be a problem. In fact he didn't seem to sense anything unusual as he opened the back door and ushered Dad, Mum, Jenny, David and Ivonia inside.

Ivonia was given her own space and from the raised positions on their parents' knees the children searched in vain for seatbelts.

"Just hold on tight," Mum hissed, and Jenny felt her Dad's arms flex around her waist as the car jolted forwards.

The town was a fascinating mixture of old and new. Many young people would not have looked out of place walking on any western high street whilst the older generation, with their long skirts and headscarves, reminded Jenny of the Babushka play they had performed at school last Christmas. Some buildings were old and drab whilst others, like the bank where they exchanged their money for Romanian lei, were new, smart, and in David's words, 'posh!"

Having been informed by Ivan that the only meal they would need to provide for themselves was breakfast, they stopped at the supermarket on the outskirts of town. Ivan noticed the look of surprise on both girls' faces.

"Ah haa!" he chortled. "You, my dear Jenny, are surprised that in Romania we have markets like your English ones. You," he turned to Ivonia, "... are surprised by all this food! It is not so in the village ... is that not true!"

Ivonia nodded and Jenny felt a tingle of excitement as she wondered what 'the village' would be like.

With large bottles of water and cartons of UHT milk squashed around their feet, Mum and Dad chatted easily to Ivan and Helena for the next hour. Ivonia answered politely when spoken to but otherwise gazed wide-eyed at Jenny, particularly fascinated by the tiny locket dangling from a thin gold chain round Jenny's neck.

"It is beautiful," she spoke suddenly, reaching out to touch the golden casing.

"My dad bought it for me on my tenth birthday," Jenny replied.

She opened the locket and showed Ivonia the two tiny pictures of herself and David and Mum and Dad, carefully cut out and positioned inside.

"I like it," Ivonia answered smiling. "But I need very big one for all my brothers and sisters to fit!"

They both laughed as the car screeched to a halt behind a horse-drawn wagon.

"We are nearly there," announced Ivan. "Next right turn and we are on our village road."

Jenny craned her neck to see. She had no idea what to expect. Dad had simply said the village was very poor and it was hoped the potato farm would become a business that would feed the villagers as well as bringing in money from selling the excess crops that weren't needed for food. Now as they turned the corner the sun came out from behind a cloud and illuminated the homes on either side of the road. Jenny shivered with anticipation. These houses were bright and modern, built in the style she had seen from the train with wooden walls, and a high fence surrounding the courtyard. It would be so exciting to live in one of these for two weeks!

But Ivan didn't stop. He continued on the mud-packed road, swerving more regularly as the number of potholes increased. Jenny clung on, gritting her teeth, whilst David grinned as if he were at last fulfilling his dream of rally driving!

The houses had changed now. They were more cramped together and some showed the same corrugated roofs Jenny had seen from the train. Ivan pulled over.

"This is our home," he announced proudly. "But before we go in I will take you to meet Ivonia's family."

He set off again.

They were still some way from Ivonia's home at the top of the road near the open farmland when Ivan pipped his horn at five eagerly waiting children. He slowed down to a steady crawl to allow them to clamber onto the bonnet and then increased his speed slightly as they hung on to each other precariously! He braked carefully as he approached the house. The children slowly slid off and formed a line, their eyes glued to the back of the car. Ivan jumped out

33

and opened the door, releasing the passengers. A lady appeared at the gate. She looked much older than Jenny's mum, although she was actually the same age. Her clothes did not show the special effort she had made to welcome these English visitors, but her smile lit her face and made everyone feel instantly at home.

"This is Nadia," introduced Ivan, "Ivonia's mum."

Nadia beckoned everybody into the living room where the table was laid with drinks and chocolate biscuits, which she handed round to the visitors before giving a nod to the anxiously waiting boys. Without hesitation Stefan, Petru and Adi dived for the plate. Chocolate biscuits were not a usual part of everyday life and they certainly meant to make the most of them!

It couldn't have been more than thirty seconds before David and the other boys disappeared outside, the thuds on the wall making it clear that they had found a football. There was a short silence as Laura, Ivonia and Jenny looked at each other. Then Laura jumped up, left the room and returned with an old battered book. She opened it and Jenny recognised immediately the Bible pictures on each page. Laura spoke to Ivonia.

"Laura says we play a game," Ivonia interpreted. "You say English word, she say Romanian."

The open book showed a picture of a beautiful garden with a man and lady peering out from behind a bush.

"Adam si Eva," Laura said slowly, nodding at Jenny for her to speak.

"Adam and Eve," announced Jenny, suddenly understanding what she was supposed to do.

The next page showed an old man with his arm round an elderly lady, who was obviously pregnant.

"Avram si Sara ..." said Laura, "... si Isaac," she added jokingly patting her stomach.

"Abraham and Sarah," repeated Jenny, "... and Isaac." She mimicked Laura's action.

They all laughed and continued their game until Ivan announced that they must go.

"We must show these people where they are going to sleep tonight," he spoke in both languages. "They will be tired. Tomorrow we come back."

Jenny was quiet as they travelled past Ivan and Helena's home. They were to stay in a small flat two miles outside the village.

"You okay love?" Mum enquired, sensing something was wrong.

"Did you see their cupboard Mum?" Jenny whispered. "The doors were off and there was nothing in it. They didn't seem to have anything!"

"I know love," Mum replied gently. "Helena says that they are one of the poorest families in the village. Their dad works hard on their plot of land, but jobs are scarce and the wages are very low. Still, they will work with Ivan and Dad on the potato project and hopefully that will improve life for them.

"But Mum!" Jenny's voice rose louder as she fought back her tears. "They had NOTHING! ... nothing ... nothing at all!"

Ivan's voice spoke softly and slowly from the front seat.

"Nothing ..." he sighed. "Nothing ... and yet they would say they had everything."

7 A long way from home

The frequent visits to grand hotels in years gone by did nothing to prepare them for their first glimpse of their accommodation.

Huge concrete blocks of flats rose depressingly out of the ground on all sides of the street. Jenny was hoping Ivan would drive straight past them to a more attractive part of the town. But those hopes were quickly dashed.

"Home for two weeks," Ivan announced, stopping the car, and Jenny was surprised that he did not apologise. Their particular block seemed to stand out bleakly from all those surrounding it. Huge lumps of concrete lay smashed on the ground round about and large cracked chunks of grey plaster clung precariously to the walls, making Jenny wary of standing beneath. What appeared to be bullet holes scattered the building's walls and old damp clothes hung drying from each window. In crevices at the base of the walls scruffy chickens clucked noisily, whilst the metallic front door swung on creaky hinges.

Jenny saw a look exchanged between her parents and heard her mum whisper:

"Oh no! John, what have we brought them to?"

Warily, they gathered their luggage.

CHAPTER SEVEN

The steps up to the first floor were gritty underfoot, due mainly to the plaster falling from the walls. Jenny could taste the dust and dirt, and the grime crunched between her teeth. Wires hung menacingly from the ceilings and stuck out of walls dangerously as Mum herded the children forward with her arms round them in protection. There was just a little light from a slit window on the first floor landing, but once they turned down a short corridor it was almost totally black. Ivan lit a match and searched for a number on a door. He fumbled in the darkness trying to fit a key in the lock. Eventually the door opened and Ivan stood back to allow the family to enter.

The tiny hall had three rooms opening off it. A door on the right led to a tiny kitchen which Mum was pleased to see contained a western oven and hob, and also a fridge. The middle door led to a small but cosy room with a table and two comfy chairs, which Ivan explained would pull out into single beds. The final door led to a bathroom which looked just like an ancient version of their bathroom at home. Mum looked relieved.

"Well at least we can have a shower and use a decent toilet ... " her voice trailed off as she saw Ivan's face.

"Not exactly," he replied. "You have water from six to eight in the morning and eight to ten at night. The rest of the time you must have buckets filled!"

He pointed to a number of buckets lined up in the bath.

"The toilet, it does not work," he continued. "You flush with bucket."

He demonstrated throwing a piece of paper into the basin and sloshing water down to force the paper along the pipes.

"You okay? I leave you and tomorrow I call at nine o'clock and take you to village."

With that he smiled, waved and clicked the door shut.

For a second Jenny thought Mum was going to cry. Dad squeezed her hand.

"Come on love," he said gently. "We'll be fine. Now who's for cocoa?"

By the time steaming cocoa and bars of chocolate were served, the lounge/bedroom looked warm and inviting. A large mat had been covered with blankets to act as a double bed, the chairs had been unfolded and bedding dragged from the top of the cupboard. Mum found some candles and they all snuggled down, Mum and Jenny in one single bed, Dad and David in another. Dad was at his best, determined to cheer them all up, especially Mum. He told tales of when he and Mum had first met and stories of Jenny and David when they were young, until they were all laughing so much that their sides began to ache and Mum had to beg him to stop!

David was almost asleep as Mum and Dad blew out the candles and crept into their mat-bed; but Jenny lay awake for a while staring into the darkness.

How could Ivonia and her family be happy with nothing? What had Ivan meant by "... they would say they have everything?" And why was it that here in a place full of dirt and poverty she had just spent the happiest night she could ever remember with her family?

Her thoughts began to blur. Her eyes closed. She fell asleep.

8 A different life

It was strange to wake up the next morning with the sun streaming through the large gap in the curtains. People were banging about in the flats above and somewhere a baby was crying. Out in the streets people were starting their cars whilst shouting greetings to their neighbours. A loud whirring noise suggested that someone nearby was doing a mechanical job.

Jenny ran to the window expecting the streets to appear different in the bright morning light - she was wrong! For as far as she could see there were nothing but grey dismal buildings, each looking identical, apart from the variety of washing hanging from the windows. Even the roads and pavements looked darker than at home, as if the sun somehow couldn't penetrate through the thin layer of grime.

Breakfast was disturbed by a loud banging on the door. David opened it and Ivan marched in beaming.

"Hello my friends. You have slept well?"

Everyone nodded sleepily.

"Tonight you sleep even better after a day in the fields! It is cold. You need warm clothes. I just go and see a friend and I come back for you in 10 minutes!"

He left and there was a rush to get ready, similar to that of a normal school day!

Mum shouted to Jenny from the bathroom:

"I think we'll take a load of those chocolate bars that Auntie Jo gave us before we left, love. And some bottles of water and some of those bats and balls—we might be in for a long day!"

Jenny rummaged through the suitcases and packed her bag full of goodies. They were ready and waiting, boots in hand, when Ivan returned.

The open farmland at the top of the village close to Ivonia's home provided an ideal place for the potato farm. The massive field spread out towards the snow-capped mountains in the north and Ivan had tested that the soil was fertile. A huge ditch, two metres wide, ran all the way along the front of the field. This had initially presented a problem, but as the soil had a tendency to become waterlogged, it had been decided that the drain they needed to fit across the middle of the field would run into the ditch, thus increasing the land's drainage. The hollow was then to be filled in with rubble, allowing vehicles to cross it. This would increase the quality of the soil but would also allow ploughs or diggers on to the land when the workers could afford them.

Ivan leapt across the ditch like a goat. The others followed, Jenny missing her footing on the far bank and slithering down the slope towards the muddy water at the bottom! Dad pulled her out, cross and filthy.

"Now you look like a real farmer," he said jokingly. "And not a very happy one!"

She frowned, sticking her tongue out at David who was doubled over laughing, and marched up the field determined that Ivan would not see how embarrassed she was.

"At least I don't have to worry about keeping clean anymore!" she mumbled bravely.

They worked hard all morning, Dad and Ivan measuring accurately the positions of drains and the dimensions of the storage barn; Jenny and David hammering in stakes of wood as markers and tying strings from one to another to show the layout of the building.

At midday they scrambled out of the field, feeling ravenous and giving no thought at all to the ditch or dirt, and walked down the road to Helena's where Mum had spent the morning painting the outside fence. She gasped when she saw Jenny.

"What on earth have you done?" she asked.

Jenny began to giggle as David retold the story of 'the slip' until all of them were laughing and tears made clean paths down Jenny's dirty face.

The workers arrived that afternoon: ten men, complete with shovels and pickaxes. Digging was frustrating work. The soil was full of clay and although Jenny and David tried their best to help they could hardly make a dint in the soil. In the end they watched until Mum arrived leading a procession of children up the road - school was over for the day!

"I've brought your rucksack Jen," Mum told her, as the children disappeared inside to change. "I've brought all these bottles of water for the workers. Thought you might like to hand out the food yourself."

Jenny undid the rucksack as Ivonia appeared.

"I've got chocolate in here from my Auntie in England," she said. "Mum says we've to feed the men."

Ivonia's eyes lit up. "Shall we make a café?" she asked. "Like Helena and Ivan take me to?"

Jenny nodded. That sounded like fun! The other children joined them a moment later and Ivonia explained the plan. Soon one area of the field had become a café. Pieces of trunks and branches were rolled into position to act as chairs. Fresh leaves were picked from nearby trees and became covers for old boxes that miraculously turned into tables! David and Stefan erected a long serving bench by jabbing forked sticks into the ground and laying long branches across them. Ana wandered happily around looking for flowers that Ivonia instructed should be on each table.

Once complete Jenny began to empty her bag and together with Laura and Ivonia arranged the drinks and chocolate on the bench.

"Ready!" announced Jenny moving the last chocolate bar into place.

"Beautiful," said Ivonia surveying their work.

Stefan shouted something and everyone except David and Jenny laughed.

"He says he will eat all that chocolate. Is there any for anyone else?" translated Ivonia.

Dad bellowed from across the field. "Hey! Are you lot ready yet? We're parched! Any chance of a drink?"

It was a lovely feast! The air was fresh and full of laughter. Mum, sitting on her log and munching a Mars bar, wondered if any stranger would have been able to distinguish, at that moment, between the two different nationalities. Each person looked hot, happy and dirty! Jenny and Ivonia could so easily have been sisters, leaning against a tree trunk, covered in mud, watching a worm wriggling its way back underground. No-one could have guessed that one child had so little in the world and the other so much.

Satisfied and refreshed, the workers resumed their work after half an hour, leaving the children to finish off any remaining chocolate.

The men continued to dig until dusk while Jenny produced a tennis ball from her rucksack pocket and Helena and Mum joined the children in a giant game of catch!

It was a sensible game to begin with until Stefan threw the ball too hard and sent it rolling into the mud at the bottom of the ditch. Adi ran to fetch it and threw it to Mum who caught it above her head sending mud splattering all over herself! The children roared with laughter, David and Jenny relieved to see that Mum seemed to find it funny!

After that the game changed into a competition as to who could get the adults the dirtiest, until the grand finale saw them all, adults included, sliding down into the bottom of the ditch in a fight to grab the ball!

As darkness began to fall, work halted and the children wandered back towards Ivonia's home. Nadia was waiting in the courtyard ready to strip the outer layers of clothing off the dripping children, placing the clothes in the tin bath to soak.

Dad looked tired as he and Mum strolled, hand in hand, down the road.

"In England a digger would have had the drains and foundations finished by now," he said. "We've hardly made a dint!"

"I know," said Mum sympathetically. "We take so much for granted."

A shout came from behind them as Ivonia and Petru caught them up.

"Petru wants to show you this," Ivonia said, as Petru pulled a bright, new, yellow tennis ball from behind his back.

"He was given this by a visitor two years ago. He has never used it as it is precious and he doesn't want it to be dirty!"

Jenny looked down at the ball in her hand. She was holding it by her fingertips as she didn't like the squidgy, soggy feel as the water oozed out from it. She held it out to Petru.

"Tell him he can have this," she said. "Now he has one clean and one dirty!"

Ivonia passed on the message and Petru's face shone as he spoke a barrage of words.

"He says may God bless you Jenny. Now he can play!" she paused shyly. "You are good and kind. You are a good friend. You are beautiful like your locket!"

She ran off quickly and left Jenny to her thoughts. How many of these balls did she have lying about in her garden at home, lost or forgotten? How strange it must be for your most precious possession to be a ball! And yet Petru wasn't sad, just delighted that now he had a dirty, soggy ball he could actually play with!

"Mum's right," she said to herself. "We do take so much for granted."

9 Gone!

The next few days flew by, the ditch was almost complete now and the huge concrete tubes needed to form the drain had been delivered and made ideal hiding places for the children! Jenny and David spent some time helping in the field, some time visiting neighbours with Mum and Helena but most of the time exploring. They loved the unstructured freedom, the chance to roam wherever they liked with no need to keep checking the time and no school or clubs to rush to. At three o'clock each afternoon Ivonia arrived home from school with her brothers and sisters and they all hurried inside to change.

The 'café' opened at the same time each day and the supplies from England were slowly being gobbled away!

Later Jenny, Laura and Ivonia would play—sometimes the book game they had played on the first day; sometimes making people out of sticks to live in home-made houses in the trees; other times they would stroll through the fields, taking Ana with them. Jenny particularly loved these times—wandering, looking at the beautiful scenery, feeling safe and relaxed without the hustle and bustle she had known all her life. Sometimes, in the surrounding peace, Amy's face would appear in her mind and she would feel momentarily sad, but she would force the thoughts away, determined to block her out completely.

Today, however, was to be different, and as Jenny looked at her reflection in the mirror, she hoped it would not be as boring as she feared.

It was Sunday and they were to go to church. Usually Jenny enjoyed church but Ivan and Helena had taken great care to explain that they would be in for a shock!

"The services are sometimes very long," Ivan had told them the previous evening. "Often they last four hours! The men and boys, they sit on one side and the women and girls on the other. Women must cover their heads. There will be no Sunday school like the English do, but Helena will translate for you."

Jenny adjusted her head scarf in the mirror. She felt silly.

"Don't worry love," Mum reassured her. "You look great and everyone else will be wearing them so you'd look sillier without one!"

Jenny felt relieved as she hadn't thought of that.

Ivan's car horn sounded outside and they ran downstairs. He looked as he had on the day they had first met, his clothes smart, his hair spiked slightly.

"Ah, you look like a true Romanian lady, my young Jenny," he said, smiling at her blushing face. "You have a notebook and pen? The service is very long; you may need something to do!"

He glanced at Mum's bulging bag and was satisfied that they were well prepared.

Helena was ready when they called in. She looked approvingly at Jenny.

"You look great," she said. "But you'll have to take your locket off! They don't like you to wear jewellery in church.

Some of the older members say it makes people look at the jewellery rather than God."

Jenny took it off rather begrudgingly and laid it on the kitchen table alongside Mum's engagement ring.

The chapel was a small wooden building built in the style of the neighbouring homes. The garden surrounding it had been lovingly cared for by members of the church.

They were greeted at the door by an elderly man. His face was wrinkled by the passage of time and the deep lines on his forehead suggested a harsh life.

Ivan put his arm around him and slapped him on the back.

"This is my dear friend Andrei!" he announced. "You will not find a better man anywhere in this world!"

Andrei spoke a few words and indicated that he wanted Ivan to translate. Ivan shook his head reluctantly but it was clear Andrei would not be happy until he was heard!

"He says 'I am his adopted child,'" Ivan explained. "He says 'I am a precious, precious son.'"

Jenny saw a look pass between Ivan and Helena. It was a strange look that Jenny couldn't understand, a look of sorrow and joy somehow all combined, but she had no time to ponder. They were quickly ushered forward.

The room was plainly decorated, the lower walls decked in wooden panels and the upper walls painted cream. Wooden pews were lined up facing the choir stalls, with a central aisle separating men and women. Andrei marched them to the front, moving Dad and David to the left, and Helena, Mum and Jenny to the right. Ivonia's family in the rows behind looked completely different, all thoroughly scrubbed and cleaned, and dressed in their smartest clothes.

Ivonia leant forward, "I come and sit with you? Yes?"

Jenny nodded, relieved to have the company.

The service was long. In fact, very long! It began with notices describing the events planned for the coming week and then moved on to warmly welcome Jenny and her family. Ivan explained about the potato project and invited helpers to join in the digging during the following week. Dad brought greetings from the church at home, explaining that many people in England were praying for the Romanian Churches. This was followed by person after person moving to the front to share a passage from the Bible that had taught them something special during the past week. Some people spoke only a few words, others many. Helena translated every word, and after the third man had gone forward to preach another sermon, Jenny wondered how she could still speak! Each person requested a favourite hymn and the congregation sang heartily as an elderly man belted out a tune on the rickety piano.

Jenny and Ivonia listened carefully for some while, but then resorted to playing noughts and crosses and drawing pictures in Jenny's notebook, until Helena announced that it was now a time of prayer and she was going to give her voice a rest. All the Romanian children immediately closed their eyes and Jenny copied them, peeping to try to spot who was praying. The prayers seemed to go on forever and Jenny was beginning to get restless when she noticed Andrei rise slowly from his chair and begin to pray. Immediately, silence fell upon the rest of the room. Each child became still, many gazing in Andrei's direction. It was as if something magical was happening. Jenny leant forward peering along her row to see if David felt it too. Yes, he too was mesmerised, as the old man continued to pray, his head lifted towards heaven, his arms slightly raised. Some people were crying, others nodding in agreement. It was obvious that something was happening, although Jenny had no idea what!

Reaching a loud crescendo, Andrei thundered "Amen!" and sat down, but Jenny couldn't take her eyes off him. Ivan saw her and winked.

The service finished shortly after, having lasted exactly 3 hours, 47 minutes and 12 seconds according to David's stopwatch! Ivan met Jenny at the door.

"Some men pray and it is as if God was here in the room," he whispered to her. "Is that not so?"

To Jenny's relief Mum rescued her from needing to answer.

"Dad's off with Ivan now love, if you want to say goodbye. Remember they're going to look at a farm project in another village. It's quite a long way so they're probably not coming back until tomorrow."

Jenny ran off to say goodbye but returned with a quizzical expression still on her face.

"You look confused love," Mum said. "I thought you would look bored after that service, not puzzled!"

"It was that man, Andrei," said Jenny, speaking her secret thoughts out loud. "It was different when he prayed. Powerful somehow. Ivan said it was because God was there. Why?"

Mum led her over to a nearby bench.

"Let me tell you something," she said, trying to choose her words carefully. "Many years ago Romania was governed by a group of people called the Communist Party. They didn't want people in this country to love God or even to believe in Him. They told people what they could and could not do and if anyone disobeyed they were in serious trouble. Andrei was the Pastor of the church in this village. He and his family had loved God for many years and when they were told to stop going to church and to stop talking about God they refused. Andrei and his sister were put in prison to teach them a lesson, but even in prison they told the guards about Jesus. His sister died in prison, but after the Communist Government was defeated, Andrei came home. He suffered so much for being a Christian it seems as if God is with him in a special way, and when he prays it's as if he was face to face with God!"

"Wow!" said Jenny quietly. "How do you know all that?"

"Helena told me," Mum answered. "She also said that one of the guards who was in charge of Andrei in prison lives in this village now!"

"Really!" said Jenny surprised. "Andrei must really hate him!"

"Apparently not ..." Mum began, but she didn't finish her sentence as Stefan ran up challenging everybody to a race home!

Helena was in the courtyard when Jenny arrived puffing and panting.

"Ivonia dropped in on her way home," she called as Jenny sped inside to collect her locket. "She said she'll come back after lunch."

"Okay," Jenny shouted back searching under the table in case her necklace had been knocked on to the floor. She couldn't see it anywhere.

"Helena have you seen my locket or Mum's ring?"

"They were on the table when I came home from church," Helena called back.

"And you're sure no one else has been here apart from Ivonia?"

Helena hurried in. "No one, just Ivonia."

'Just Ivonia.' Those words rang in Jenny's mind. A feeling of horror and anger began to rise inside her. She remembered the way Ivonia had looked at the locket, the way she had touched it and described its beauty. The temptation must have been too great for her—she must have taken it! It couldn't have been anyone else! Jenny sat down. How dare she, after all those words about being a special friend? Well she would show her! She didn't need friends like that. Just wait till the afternoon!

10 The accusation

Jenny was waiting by the gate ready to pounce on Mum the moment she returned from church.

"Mum, you didn't move your ring or my locket did you, before we went to church? Helena said she'd seen them, but she could be wrong!"

"No love," Mum answered looking puzzled. "They were on the table last time I saw them. Why?"

"They've gone Mum!" Jenny blurted out beginning to sob. "They've gone and no one's been here, apart from Ivonia!"

Mum hurried inside and together they moved the furniture and lifted rugs. The search was unsuccessful.

"Could they have been stolen when we were at church?" Mum called into the kitchen where Helena was busily preparing lunch.

Helena appeared, looking upset and flustered. "I know they were here when I came home," she said with certainty. "I picked up the locket and looked at it before I began to make lunch."

"Then it has to be Ivonia!" Jenny blurted out again. "No one else called round."

"Jenny! Ivonia would never do that!" Helena looked as if she was close to tears. "She is a good girl, with a good heart. She would not steal. No never!"

She returned quickly to the kitchen wiping her eyes. Jenny turned to Mum, anger in her face.

"She loved that locket, Mum. She was always looking at it. I know it's her! She must've taken your ring, because if she had only taken the locket, it would have made it even more obvious that it was her!"

"Come and sit down love," Mum spoke firmly and Jenny sat down obediently. "You can't go accusing Ivonia of something like this! You have no proof she stole it. She seems honest and you've been such good friends."

"Not any more," muttered Jenny under her breath. Mum and Helena may be willing to give her the benefit of the doubt, but she would not! She knew she was right!

Lunch was a silent affair. Jenny ate little and spoke even less.

It was as Helena cleared away the plates that the creaking of the gate cut through the stillness and Ivonia appeared in the doorway.

She had changed from her 'Sunday best' clothes and once again wore the usual track suit and t-shirt.

"I said I would return after lunch," she announced, smiling round, unconscious of the cold atmosphere. "If you are still eating, I will go away and come back later."

"No, you're fine," said Helena, looking uncomfortable.

"You come for a walk, Jenny?" Ivonia continued. "I tell Ana we maybe go with her ... if you like."

Jenny stood up. She had calmed down a little during lunchtime and had decided to talk to Ivonia in a grown-up manner. Now, however, with Ivonia standing smiling across the room, her anger began to well up again.

"How dare she act as if nothing was wrong!" she muttered through gritted teeth.

She was just like Amy, pretending she wasn't rich and making Jenny feel so silly. Now here was Ivonia pretending she hadn't pinched the locket! What was it about her so called 'friends' that made them always try to deceive her? Did they think she was stupid? Well she had had enough!

She moved coldly towards Ivonia, her eyes flashing.

"How dare you?" she roared, finding herself trembling. "You pretend to be such a goodie goodie; you pretend you don't mind being poor and all the time you're plotting to steal my locket as soon as you get a chance! And, as if that wasn't enough, you take Mum's ring too!"

She paused to catch her breath.

"Jenny, stop it!" demanded Mum. "Give Ivonia a chance to speak!"

But Jenny would not stop.

"You aren't my friend!" she hissed. "You are nothing but a little thief! I don't care if I never see you again!"

Ivonia looked completely shocked. She opened her mouth, but found herself unable to speak so let it close slowly. She gazed round the room bewildered, before turning to glance back at Jenny as she fled, uttering a few words in Romanian.

"What did she say?!" demanded Jenny.

"She said she knows nothing about your locket ..." translated Helena, finding it difficult to speak. "... and that she would never hurt a friend like you!"

She left the room but Jenny could hear her sniffing in the kitchen and realised she had gone too far.

"You shouldn't have spoken like that." Mum's voice
rang with disappointment. "You need to apologise to both
Ivonia and Helena."

Jenny shrugged her shoulders. She might apologise
to Helena but there was no way she was saying sorry
to Ivonia. After all, it was her fault; she had stolen the
necklace and it was she who needed to apologise!

Jenny had a miserable afternoon. David disappeared to
play football with some local boys. Mum and Helena sat
darning socks and mending a wide variety of clothes for
elderly neighbours. Jenny sat beside the window, listening
to the laughter of children enjoying a day of freedom away
from school. She desperately wanted to join them but she
was sure she wouldn't be welcome. By now there had been
plenty of time for Ivonia to tell the entire village about her
accusation, and no doubt, they would all believe her side of
the story, making Jenny out to be the villain.

She blinked her eyes to try to clear the mist from in
front of them. It just wasn't fair! She wiped away a tear
running down her cheek and saw Helena watching her
from across the room. She turned away ashamed. Why had
all this happened to her again? She wasn't a bad person.
After all, she went to church each week, tried to be good,
tried to be patient with her brother, even when he was a
complete pain! Maybe she was just rubbish at making or
at least keeping friends. Maybe she would just be lonely
and friendless for the rest of her life.

They left Helena's house before tea. Mum said they
were tired and needed a rest, but everyone knew the
real reason. All the joy of the holiday had disappeared.
The atmosphere felt broken and awkward and Helena

kept wringing her hands together, unsure of what to do. Eventually she summoned a neighbour to drive the family home in the hope that the well-known saying might be true and things really would 'seem better in the morning!'

11 Dad's return

Jenny was glad when dawn broke. Even in the dismal, grey, dirty streets the birds began to twitter their beautiful morning chorus.

She had slept fitfully, tossing and turning, dreaming of Ivonia and Amy and waking occasionally to find the pillow wet with tears. Wandering into the kitchen she found Mum sitting on a wooden stool, warming her hands around a mug of tea. The dark shadows under her eyes and the lines furrowed in her forehead suggested that she too had had a night of worry and little sleep.

She looked up as Jenny entered the room, her eyes still full of sadness and disappointment.

"I am sorry, Mum!" Jenny snapped. "But you've always told us that stealing is wrong! If she'd just own up then I'd forgive her and be friends again!"

"Oh Jenny," Mum said sadly, leaning her head in her hands. "Jenny, what if it wasn't her? You shouldn't have accused her like that. You lost your temper with Amy and spoilt that friendship, and now you've done it again."

"Mum!" Jenny yelled. "I can't believe you're taking their side against me! Ivonia must have taken my locket; there was no one else there to do it ... unless it was Helena ..." Her voice trailed off.

Mum glowered at her.

"Don't you dare accuse her!" she spoke in a quiet, exasperated growl that made Jenny quickly decide not to argue.

"Helena has been so kind to us," Mum continued. "You owe her a huge apology, never mind branding her a thief as well!"

Jenny felt a sudden pang of guilt. She knew deep down that Helena wouldn't steal, but if anyone had asked her the day before, she'd have said that Ivonia would never steal anything either ... and now she definitely had! A tiny doubt crept into Jenny's mind. She remembered the look of shocked surprise on Ivonia's face when she had called her a thief; she remembered the look of deep hurt in her eyes as she turned and ran away. Was she really such a good actress? What if ... what if she was wrong ...? Jenny swallowed hard; she couldn't bear to think about it.

"I'm going in the shower," she muttered, relieved to lock herself away from everyone for a short while.

Jenny closed her eyes and let the lukewarm water sprinkle over her face. If she was wrong, if Ivonia hadn't taken the locket and there was some other explanation for its disappearance, then their friendship was over. Ivonia would hate her forever and quite rightly too! Jenny remembered her own fury when a teacher had wrongly accused her of cheating in a spelling test; she had even apologised later and told Jenny she had made a mistake, but Jenny had disliked that teacher ever since.

She screwed her eyes together more tightly, trying to blot out the two faces that lingered so vividly in her mind. Ivonia, her eyes puzzled and full of shock and hurt;

Amy, a bewildered look spreading across her face, not understanding why Jenny should be so mad with her.

How she wished the water could simply wash away the faces along with the pain she felt inside.

An enormous BANG broke into her thoughts. She jumped, the water stopped and Mum's voice echoed through the air.

"David! What on earth have you done now?!"

Jenny climbed, shivering from the bath, wrapped a towel around herself and hurried into the hallway to find Mum peering into the box containing the electric meter.

"David's managed to blow all the electrics," she muttered, looking even less pleased than before.

"I didn't mean to," David snapped. "All I did was put the kettle and grill on at the same time and there was that almighty BANG! I was actually trying to make breakfast to try to cheer everyone up!"

Mum looked guilty now. "Okay, okay," she said. "It doesn't matter. We've obviously overloaded the system. We'll have to wait until Dad gets back, he may be able to fix it."

It was a quiet, awkward morning waiting for Helena's neighbour to collect them. Mum tided up, Jenny pretended to read and David played on his Nintendo. He only once tried to lighten the atmosphere, by suggesting that they could all play a game of 'Happy Families', but scowls from both Mum and Jenny silenced him abruptly and he busied himself trying to beat his highest score.

At 11 o'clock they were ready and waiting outside the front door as their lift pulled up. Jenny had practiced her apology to Helena over and over in her mind. She was determined to get it out of the way immediately, and as the car arrived outside Helena's home, Jenny jumped out and hurried inside.

Helena was standing in the small, cosy kitchen as usual, making lunch. Jenny ran over and threw her arms round her.

"I'm sorry Helena," she blurted out. "I was rude and I shouldn't have been. I really am sorry!"

Helena looked down at her and stroked her head.

"Thank you Jenny for saying that. But it is Ivonia you need to talk to. Laura called here this morning and said Ivonia was crying all last night. She is very unhappy."

"Well so am I!" grumbled Jenny. "If she hadn't taken my locket none of this would've happened."

Helena's eyes clouded over again.

"Jenny," she said gently. "You are wrong. I don't know where that locket is but I trust Ivonia completely."

A car door banged shut on the road.

"Dad's here!!" screeched David.

Everyone raced outside. Jenny hurled herself at Dad, clinging to him as if she would never let go.

Ivan wrapped his arms around his wife, aware of the firmness of her grasp and the slight trembling of her body. He knew something was wrong.

"It seems," announced Ivan, looking both pleased and confused, "that they cannot manage without us!"

Dad also appeared rather overwhelmed by the welcome.

"I think I need to go away more often ..." he chortled to himself. "They're not usually so pleased to see me ..." He stopped abruptly when he saw Mum's frown.

"Come on," he said more seriously, loosening Jenny's grip on him. "Looks like you've got a lot to tell us. Let's go inside."

He headed towards the door, turned and put his hand in his pocket.

"Before you tell us what's going on, let me just give these back to you," he said. "I picked them up off the kitchen table when we called in for Ivan's bag after church yesterday. Thought they might get pinched or something as they were in full view of the door."

He opened his clasped hands.

There, in his open palm, glinting in the sunlight, lay a ring and a beautiful golden locket!

Mum, Helena, David and Jenny gasped. Any remaining colour drained from Jenny's face.

There was a pause as Dad and Ivan tried to understand the reaction.

Complete horror gripped every part of Jenny's being. Her locket! Her locket that she was so certain Ivonia had stolen. And yet here it was lying in Dad's hand! She was wrong! She had done it again ... ruined a friendship and called Ivonia a thief.

She let out a bloodcurdling sob, threw her hands up to her face and fled out of the gate along the muddy road. She had to get away!

12 Hidden secret

How Jenny found her way to the large tree trunk at the far end of the potato field she never knew; nor had she any idea how long someone had quietly been sitting beside her waiting for the sobbing to subside. All she knew was that when she eventually did open her red, swollen eyes, there sat Ivan watching her closely. He moved closer once she had seen him and placed his arm around her, and she in turn laid her head upon his shoulder and wept again.

When she lifted her head he handed her a tissue and spoke softly.

"I know all about it Jenny. Helena has told me everything."

Jenny shrugged her shoulders. "So now you've come to tell me how stupid I am and how I must apologise to Ivonia and that I need to learn to keep my temper."

Ivan shook his head.

"No Jenny," he said, thinking carefully about his words. "I've come to tell you that you made a mistake, but that God loves you very much."

Jenny looked at him quizzically; this was not what she had expected at all!

"God can't really love me," she said sadly. "I know you think he can but you don't really know me. I mess everything up. It's not just Ivonia … I lose every friend I ever have."

She gazed across to the mountains. They seemed so far away, their summits tipped with snow; but her thoughts wandered further away still, to Amy's garden and the hurtful, cutting words she had spoken. And suddenly, unexpectedly, the whole story tumbled out of her mouth in a jumble that she was sure Ivan could not understand but that she was glad to release anyway.

"… and so," she concluded, "… I was so angry that she had so much more than me and her house was so huge and she'd pretended she liked my house even though it was miles smaller than hers. She made me look so stupid and I was so jealous and I called her some horrid, horrid names …" her voice trailed off.

"And were you right about her, Jenny?" Ivan asked quietly, "Had she kept quiet about how rich she was or what a lovely house she had just to make you look silly?"

Jenny thought for a moment. She knew the truth. She'd known the truth all along but had been afraid to admit it.

"No," she said with certainty. "I think she really did like my house. I don't think she cared if it was big or small. I think she wanted to give me a nice surprise about her house and share her garden and swimming pool with me … but I was too jealous to see."

Ivan nodded again, "And what about Ivonia?"

"I jumped to the wrong conclusion again," Jenny whispered. "I thought she must have taken the locket because there was no other explanation … I thought she must be jealous of me like I was of Amy … but she wasn't, even though she has hardly anything in the world … I should've stopped and realised that she wouldn't do that to me ... Oh Ivan! What am I going to do?"

She burst into tears again; this time not tears of self-pity but tears of real sorrow, from a heart that was sorry for what had been done and longed to be able to turn the clock back and make things right.

"You must say sorry," said Ivan without hesitation. "You must go to them and asked them to forgive you, and Jenny, maybe you need to ask God to forgive you too."

Jenny gazed out over the fields. She'd been to church week after week all her life and she had heard many times that God could forgive anything wrong she had done, but it had never really struck her that she had to do anything about it.

"Ivan," she turned to look directly at him. "Ivan, maybe God will forgive me, but Ivonia and Amy won't. You didn't hear what I said. You didn't see how I hurt them. They won't ever forgive me."

It was Ivan's turn now to gaze across to the mountains. When he spoke his words were so firm and sure that Jenny was slightly shocked.

"Jenny ... when the love of God is in someone's heart they have the power to forgive no matter what a person has done to them."

"But Ivan," Jenny insisted, "it's so easy for you to say that. You're so nice. Everyone likes you. I bet you've never needed forgiveness from anyone in your whole life!"

It seemed like minutes until Ivan spoke again. When he did speak his eyes were brimming with tears and his voice was choked.

"Jenny ... do you remember Andrei, my dear friend at church?"

"Yes," said Jenny, suddenly hoping that she may be about to find out the answer to a question in her mind. "Mum told me he had been in prison because he wouldn't stop following God, and she said one of his guards lived in the village ... I said, 'he must really hate him' ... I'd love to know who he was!"

"And do you remember, Jenny," Ivan continued, "what Andrei said about me?"

"Yes," said Jenny, wondering where the conversation was taking them. "He called you 'his precious son.'"

"So you'd say he loved me then?" Ivan asked, turning to face her.

Jenny nodded.

"So you'd say he had forgiven and even loved the man that laughed at him, hit him and spat in his face?"

His words trailed off as the realisation of what Ivan was saying dawned upon Jenny.

"It was ... it was you?" she stuttered. "You were Andrei's guard?"

Ivan nodded. "Yes," he whispered. "I'm ashamed to say it was me, Jenny ... But Jenny," he gave a watery smile ... "Thank God! My life was changed by the power of forgiveness!"

13 Ivan's story

Ivan remained deep in thought, as if his mind had travelled to some old, forgotten, unhappy world.

Jenny was unsure of what to say but she was bursting with questions and eventually she could hold them in no longer.

"Ivan, will you tell me about it?" she asked, her voice cutting through the silence. "Tell me what happened. How come Andrei doesn't hate you?"

Ivan sighed. "Jenny, most people in this village do not know about my past. Andrei wanted it to be like that as he was afraid that not everyone could forgive and forget as he can. What I will tell you is a hidden secret. Your Mum knows all about it from Helena, but few others know."

Jenny smiled. "I'm good with secrets," she said eagerly.

Ivan began to tell his story, his eyes full of regret and his voice so soft that Jenny had to strain her ears to hear him.

"When I was young," he whispered, "I was full of love for my country and my Romanian people. I joined the government's Young Communist Party with great enthusiasm. I learnt that I didn't need God and that, in fact, there was no God. I learnt that to obey the government and to fight against anyone who did not obey them was the most important thing a person could do in his life. Before long I became a guard in a local prison. There were a few men in there who had committed serious crimes, but many were imprisoned because they were leaders of churches who refused to stop following God, even though the government said that they must. As guards we would laugh at these men. To us they were stupid, all they had to do was to stop talking about Jesus and they could go free ... but they would not stop ... in fact they talked about Jesus all the time ... sometimes I wanted to listen ... I could not understand how they could believe in God when they were wasting their lives in prison."

Ivan glanced at Jenny, saw that she was gripped by the story, and continued.

"One day we had been told to interrogate a particular man. We were to try to force him to say that there was no God and that he would never speak of him again. We tried for hour after hour, but he would not give in. He just looked at us and said he would follow his God forever. I became more and more angry, until I could listen to him no longer! I rounded on him. I hit him very hard and... I spat in his face ..."

Ivan paused, struggling for words.

"... I will never forget what he said... he looked me directly in the eyes. There was no hate there. He simply said, 'Ivan, God loves you and I forgive you.'"

Ivan paused again, seeming to feel the impact of those words afresh.

"Jenny, those words burnt deep into my heart and I never forgot them. I didn't believe in God so I had no idea whether or not he loved me, but I knew from the look in

Andrei's eyes that he had forgiven me for all my cruelty, and I couldn't escape from that!"

"So what happened?" asked Jenny. "How did you become such good friends?"

"Two years later," Ivan continued, "many things changed in this country. The government was overthrown and many religious prisoners were released. I continued to be a prison guard, but no matter what I did or where I went Andrei's words seemed to follow me. Then one day I was walking past a church and I heard singing. Something made me go inside and a man at the front talked about God sending his son Jesus to die on a cross in our place so we could be forgiven for all the wrong things we had done. He explained that Jesus had lived a perfect life but had been punished instead of us and, if we were really sorry, God would forgive us and make us like new people."

Suddenly the sun appeared from behind a cloud and a bright ray of sunshine fell on the tree trunk, illuminating Ivan and Jenny. Ivan lifted his head and smiled.

"It was just like that!" he laughed. "A light shone into my heart. I went to the front of the church, knelt down and cried as I asked God to forgive me, make me clean and give me a new life. I left the church a different man! My heart was light. I skipped down the road! I remember a group of boys standing at the corner laughing at me as I skipped; but I did not care! I was free!"

Jenny laughed too as Ivan continued.

"I knew God had forgiven me, but in my heart I knew I needed to ask forgiveness from the man whom I had hurt so much but whose words had changed my life. I knew which village Andrei came from and guessed he had returned there. So I went to find him. I turned into the village road praying that God would lead me to someone who knew the way to Andrei's house. And there, walking down the middle of the road was Andrei himself! I stopped the car and ran to meet him. He was taken aback at first, unsure who I was, and then suddenly he recognised me!

'Ivan?' he whispered.

I knelt at his feet in the mud and asked his forgiveness. He took hold of my hand, lifted me to my feet, hugged me and said ..." Ivan's voice trailed off and he swallowed a few times struggling for words.

"... he said, 'Welcome home my precious son.' From then on I lived in his home with him and his wife. My past was forgotten. I was free and loved and forgiven. I met Helena and told her all about my life, she accepted me as I was and Andrei married us in the village church... he said it was the proudest day of his life."

Ivan glanced at Jenny who had gone strangely silent.

"You know, Jenny," he whispered. "Ivonia has the same love of God in her heart. I'm sure she will forgive you."

He stood up. "I will leave you for a while. Now you know my hidden secret, but remember Jenny, there are no secrets hidden from God. He knows all things, but he still loves you."

He walked away and Jenny smiled as she saw him take a few skips at the edge of the field.

Ivan's story had given her hope. Maybe Ivonia would forgive; but that wasn't the main thought in her mind just now. She raised her head to the sky where the sun was now just a dull glow behind the clouds.

"God," she prayed out loud, unafraid of anyone hearing. "God please will you forgive me and make me a new person like you did with Ivan. I don't want to be jealous and angry anymore and I can't change on my own; but if you can change Ivan then I think maybe you can change me! Amen."

Suddenly the sun appeared again, lighting up Jenny's face in the same way as a beam of happiness seemed to be illuminating her heart.

She sprang off the log and skipped across the field. She knew what she had to do and she wasn't going to waste any time!

14 Forgiven

"Helena!" Jenny shouted at the top of her voice, as she dashed past her surprised Mum and Dad and burst into the kitchen.

"Helena, please will you come with me to Ivonia's house? It's just, I know her English is good but I really need her to understand that I really am sorry ... and I need you to explain things to her mum!"

Helena stopped. She had been in the kitchen since Ivan had set off in search of Jenny, praying and busying herself with any little job that could take her mind away from worrying. Now, looking down at Jenny's dirty, tearstained face, she sensed something important had happened and hurriedly removed her apron and followed Jenny back outside.

Most of the journey to Ivonia's home was made in silence; firstly, because Jenny was playing over and over in her mind exactly what she wanted to say, and secondly, because they were walking so quickly that neither of them had enough breath to speak!

It was as Ivonia's small, wooden house came into view that Jenny slowed the pace slightly and turned towards Helena.

"Helena?" she panted, conscious that she was becoming more nervous with every step they took towards Ivonia's home. "Helena, I really am sorry. I've asked God to forgive me, but please, please will you help me make Ivonia forgive me too?"

"Jenny," Helena replied, "I can't make Ivonia do anything. All you can do is to ask someone for forgiveness. It is up to them if they are willing to forgive."

They stopped outside the small wooden gate and, mustering all her courage, Jenny pressed down the latch, walked slowly across the courtyard and knocked on the door.

Nadia appeared, her apron covered in flour from the morning's bread making. She saw Jenny's face and nodded towards the parlour door, sensing that the two girls would need time together.

Jenny had never been in the parlour before. Nervousness and cold seem to rack her whole body. The room was dark and damp but the sun seemed to stream in a single ray through the small window that fell upon an old picture hanging on the wall. It showed a man in a long white dress sitting on a rock. Gathered around his feet sat children from all over the world. Their hair, their skin, their clothes were all different; some looked rich, some looked poor; but the man, who Jenny assumed was Jesus, had his arms open wide, as if he was pulling every child towards him.

The click of the door closing made Jenny jump. There stood Ivonia, her head bowed forward, gazing at the bare floorboards.

Jenny had practised and practised her speech but, seeing Ivonia before her looking so sad, she forgot all the words.

CHAPTER FOURTEEN

"Ivonia," she choked, "I'm so, so sorry. I was completely wrong. I know you wouldn't take anything. I thought you were jealous like me and ... Oh Ivonia! I was wrong! Please forgive me!"

It was Jenny's turn now to study the floor, scared to lift her eyes to Ivonia's in case she would not forgive.

She heard the floorboards creak and then felt two gentle hands take hold of her own. She raised her head to find Ivonia smiling, her eyes showing the same look as Ivan had seen in Andrei's.

"I forgive you," Ivonia said with such ease and certainty that Jenny was left in no doubt about the truth of her answer. "We all make mistakes Jenny, but remember I am not jealous. God has given me so much and I am happy with what I have!"

Jenny nodded. She couldn't understand it properly but she knew Ivonia spoke the truth. She had nothing, but Ivan had been completely right, she had everything. She had discovered so young that money and possessions could never bring lasting peace and happiness to her heart, but that love, for God and family and friends, could bring joy even in poverty.

She glanced again at the picture on the wall and for a moment saw herself and Ivonia sitting there at Jesus' feet: one rich and one poor, but He loved and accepted them both just the same.

"Ivonia," Jenny asked suddenly, "will you come for a walk with me?"

Ivonia nodded and the two girls left the house hand-in-hand.

Looking out of the window Nadia and Helena smiled. Helena had explained everything, and despite Ana's desperate pleas to be allowed to go walking with the girls, Nadia decided that they needed to be alone.

Jenny never told Ivonia about Ivan's hidden secret; she had said she wouldn't and she knew that it was Ivan's choice whom he told. She did however tell Ivonia all about asking God to forgive and change her, as they sat back on the tree trunk in the potato field.

Ivonia turned to her, eyes shining and happy.

"Now we both follow Jesus," she announced. "We are not just best friends, we are like sisters!"

*   *   *

Jenny thought about the day as she lay in bed that night. What a difference a day could make! Last night she had been full of anger and sadness, tonight she felt as if she could explode with happiness. Even thoughts of Amy couldn't dampen her spirits. She remembered again Helena's words: "All you can do is to ask someone for forgiveness. It is up to them if they are willing to forgive."

She would do that when she got home. If Amy wouldn't forgive then that was her choice - but she would say sorry and mean it. For now though, she would just enjoy the rest of the holiday!

She shut her eyes and slept in peace.

15 Snowfall

There was a strange chill in the air as Jenny tucked the blankets more tightly around her body in an attempt to keep warm.

The early morning light shining through the curtains gave off a brighter, more mysterious glow than usual. David recognised it at once and leaped out of bed.

"Wow, you lot! Come and look at this!" he shouted, throwing wide the curtains and gazing in excitement into the street below.

Jenny sprang up, keeping the blanket firmly wrapped around her shoulders.

The streets were no longer dirty and dull but clean and white, in stark contrast to the greyness of the buildings that remained unchanged except for thin, white, horizontal stripes where the snow had collected along the balconies.

They were outside in a flash, jumping in the fresh, thick blanket of powdery snow—so deep it spilt over the tops of their boots and made their toes wet and tingly. They had never seen snow like this! In England they'd seen little more than a thin layer of white, just enough to scrape together a small snowman and throw a few snowballs. But this snow was deep and luscious, so soft you could fall back on to it like a comfy cushion. Even when David threw a snowball directly into Jenny's face it didn't hurt, but broke instantaneously into tiny flakes that melted and dribbled down her neck.

They played enthusiastically for half an hour and then scurried upstairs to thaw out and collect a warm drink. They were disappointed!

The electricity had still not been reconnected and they were relieved to answer a knock at the door and find Ivan waiting outside.

"Helena said I must come early," he announced. "She said you will be cold with no electricity and no wood for the heater."

He nodded towards Jenny and David huddled freezing in the corner.

"I think she is right!" he laughed.

The trip to the village was hazardous. Ivan seemed to take little account of the weather and drove at his normal speed. Jenny noticed Mum's eyes were firmly closed and was certain that she wasn't sleeping!

It seemed strange to Jenny that so much snow could have so little effect on everyday life. Everyone seemed to be going about their normal business, having simply added a few more layers of clothing and walking more briskly. She thought of England where a splattering of snow would cause chaos and even close schools.

"Will the school be shut today Ivan?" she suddenly asked anxiously.

Ivan laughed.

"You are not in England now my little Jenny," he said, turning round and making the car swerve violently towards a ditch! He corrected it and turned round again.

"Do not worry. Nothing will shut the school. The children may be late. They will have to dig out all their old neighbours. But snow is not so big a thing for us as it is for you."

Jenny was relieved. She had work to do today. Helena had arranged to take herself, David and Mum to visit the local school. Jenny's head teacher in England had asked her to take photographs and to give a talk about life in a Romanian school when she returned home. Jenny loved doing things like that and she was determined to make a good job of it.

Helena had been up early and the delicious smell of homemade bread filled the house and seemed to filter through the walls to the children the minute they clambered out of the car. They ran inside to find a table laden with freshly baked bread, butter, cheese and jugs of steaming tea and hot blackcurrant. The heaters were roasting and Jenny and David huddled against them, enjoying the feel of the heated tiles along the whole length of their bodies.

They had almost thawed out when Laura, Ivonia and Stefan appeared in the doorway.

"I thought you might like a bit of company on your way to school," Helena said, nodding towards them. "And I thought they might like a bit of breakfast!"

Stefan walked forward, grinned and made a motion with his arm as if he were throwing a ball across the room. David immediately pretended to fall backwards acting as if it had smashed into his face and was now making him very cold. Everyone understood and laughed!

"Stefan, you can play snowballs with David as soon as you finish breakfast ... but not until then!" Helena said firmly. "... and don't get too wet before school!"

Ivonia and Jenny exchanged glances and rolled their eyes. Jenny was pleased Helena had asked them. She had felt just a bit uneasy about meeting Ivonia today. She wasn't sure if she ought to say sorry a few more times, or just to act as if nothing had happened. But somehow Stefan and David acting silly made everything normal again and Jenny felt suddenly glad she had a brother, even if he drove her mad most of the time!

Work at the potato field had been abandoned for the day. Dad and Ivan were to spend the time locating the cheapest places to buy the remainder of the materials needed for the building.

After breakfast Helena decreed that there were 45 minutes before they must set off to school, so Laura, Ivonia and Jenny sneaked out of the house. No words had been exchanged but each knew where they were going.

"Beat you there!" shouted Ivonia, and they all ran.

The potato field lay undisturbed. Ivan had been there just after dawn but had resisted the temptation to trample all over it. He remembered the thrill he had felt as a child when he had arrived at fields of unbroken whiteness and had been the first to plant his footprints in the snow. No doubt, he thought, later that day the children of the village would be hoping for the same experience and he left it perfectly intact.

The three girls stopped abruptly at the edge of the field, taken aback by the beauty spread before them. In the distance the mountains rose like huge white giants, shimmering and glinting in the sun; closer to them the sunlight danced off the brilliant snow, its reflection forcing them to squint through half-shut eyes. Only the trees, their branches still brown and bare from winter, seemed to stand out against the white background. Occasional gentle groans and haunted creaks added an eerie feel to the still air, as the heavily laden branches struggled to bear the weight of snow piled upon them.

"It's so beautiful!" Jenny whispered. "I don't want to spoil it!"

Laura and Ivonia nodded in agreement. They waited in silence for two or three minutes and simultaneously turned to set off home, unwilling to make even one mark on the smooth, flat surface.

They had taken about 10 paces down the road when a terrific noise announced the arrival of the boys thundering their way towards them. There was no way they were going to stop to admire the scenery; and there was no way the girls would allow them to break the surface before them!

Laura, Ivonia and Jenny turned round in panic!

"RUN!" they all screeched at once.

It was hard to run in the thick snow but the girls reached the field first. This time they did not stop to look round but dived full-length over the boundary, disappearing for a few seconds and then appearing again covered in snow!

The boys followed. Diving and burrowing tunnels like moles under the crispy surface, popping up unexpectedly with small mounds of snow on their heads! They ran and leapt, rolling over and over, churning up the surface without a care in the world. Stefan shouted across to Ivonia.

"He says we will play 'snow head' tig!" she translated. "Stefan's on. He collects a big snowball or chunk of snow and when he smashes it over someone's head that person is the catcher instead!"

David grinned. This was his kind of game!

The wild feeling of fun and freedom continued until David pointed across the field to where Dad and Ivan were madly waving.

"Helena says it is time for school," Ivan shouted clearly, first in Romanian and then in English.

The children giggled as automatically each one lifted their hands to their ears pretending to be unable to hear, forcing Dad and Ivan to walk across to them! Neither man could resist taking a fresh path through the snow and they were too busy talking to hear both David and Stefan cry out a half-hearted warning:

"MIND THE DITCH!"

It was too late! Suddenly both Dad and Ivan disappeared as if by magic and the children ran over to drag them out soaking wet and totally white, but laughing hysterically!

A huge snowball fight followed—men against children —until Ivan convinced them that Helena may refuse to make them any food for the rest of the day if they didn't return when she had ordered. The thought of that made them all flee in panic—they were already hungry!

Both Mum and Helena pretended to be cross when the dripping company of men and children sneaked guiltily into the house.

"Men always turn into boys again when the snow comes!" Helena complained in a frustrated voice, trying to avoid Ivan hugging her in his wet clothes.

"They never seem to grow up! Anyway you children get yourselves dry. It is time for school!"

16 School-life

*I*t seemed to Jenny that most of the school children were late. They sauntered to their classrooms chattering and laughing as they would in England, but without any sense of urgency or awareness of the time.

The school consisted of two brick buildings. The Lower School housed children aged six to twelve years and the Upper School those aged thirteen and upwards. Helena ushered them through the Lower School towards the reception classroom, where the teacher welcomed them warmly.

It was a large dark room with high windows that allowed in little light. Faded posters were dotted at regular intervals round the walls and worn, dusty plastic flowers decorated the teacher's desk. The children sat cross-legged on a rug listening intently as an assistant read to them from an old tatty book. They peered round when the visitors entered, nudging each other excitedly.

One little girl sprang up and ran over to the book, speaking rapidly in Romanian. She pointed frantically at a picture and then at Jenny. All the children gasped, staring wide eyed at her, making Jenny feel extremely uncomfortable.

"She say you look like princess in story," laughed the teacher, in broken English. "She say you wear dress like this in England ... yes ... no?"

Jenny walked over and looked at the picture. She recognised the story of Cinderella instantly, her sequined ball gown still looking stunning despite the faded pages.

She shook her head. "I have no dress like that," she said, thinking of her bedroom at home with its wardrobe full of clothes. She knew the idea of Cinderella and Prince Charming was merely a fairytale, but she wondered what these children would say if they could see her home and all her possessions; surely that would seem like a fairytale to them!

The teacher clapped her hands and directed the children to the shelving that lined the walls. They moved slowly and reluctantly, collecting battered games and jigsaws to play with. It was obvious that they were not at all interested in such things this morning. Mum had placed two large plastic bags next to the door and every pair of mischievous eyes was keeping watch, determined not to miss a treat!

Seeing their faces, Mum nodded towards the door and Jenny and David collected a bag each. They were immediately surrounded!

In the week before their trip Jenny and her family had been surprised by the number of people who had called at their house bearing gifts that they hoped may be used either in the Romanian schools or by the village children. They had been inundated with school equipment, toys, games, stickers, sweets and many other presents. It now seemed that the struggle to cram everything into the suitcases had been worthwhile.

Jenny lifted the equipment out one piece at a time: jigsaws, number games, counting blocks, toy cars, picture books, felt pens, rulers, even a stop watch. She handed them to the children. There was no grabbing, no complaining that anyone wanted something different. Each child held their gift tightly on their knees, fingering the boxes and sniffing the smell of newness. Most of them had never received anything new. The charity vans came regularly, bringing with them an adequate collection of used toys; but new things, with no tears on the boxes and no faded, bent edges on the books, were an unknown novelty.

All too quickly the teacher ordered that the new equipment be piled on the table for future use, and recognising the children's disappointment, David began to undo his bag.

This bag was different! This wasn't equipment to be used in school when the teacher allowed. This was a bag full of small gifts, enough for each child. Jenny and David had had great fun collecting them; bouncy balls, bubbles, gliders, sequined purses, whoopee cushions and more. This time the children couldn't sit still! They crowded round, each trying to push closer so they could make their choice. What followed was complete chaos! Bouncy balls and gliders cascaded round the room. In the far corner a boy and girl rolled about laughing, tears streaming down their faces, as they took turns to blow up and sit on the whoopee cushion, sending rude noises vibrating through the air!

After ten minutes Helena suggested that maybe they should leave, to allow the teacher to regain some form of control. They were to visit Ivonia and Stefan's classroom next, where Helena had arranged a question and answer session so Jenny could collect the information she needed for her talk.

Ivonia grinned and waved at Jenny as they entered the room. Stefan waggled his fingers in his ears and stuck his tongue out at David, who copied him and received a ferocious glare from Mum.

This room was also dark and felt much colder than the first classroom. The desks reminded Jenny of a Victorian school room she had once seen in a museum. The benches were made out of wood and could seat two or three people. They were attached by metal frames to long, dark, wooden, hinged desks. Faded green velvet cloths had been placed over each desk, although one or two had been peeled back to make room for notebooks and pencils.

The teacher's table and chair were positioned in one corner, a clean blackboard stood at the front and two pictures of distinguished gentlemen hung on the walls. A row of empty pegs lined one wall as the children huddled into their coats and pulled bobble hats round their ears. The usual brown tiled heater remained stone cold. Helena explained that the school could only afford to heat the classrooms of the youngest children, except in the depths of winter.

The children were eager not only to answer Jenny's questions but also to ask their own. They asked about the weather, houses, schools, the queen, shops, cars and especially football!

Bit by bit Jenny pieced together the answers to her own questions:

- There were 127 pupils in the school.
- This was the only school in the village.
- The children went to the local school until the age of sixteen. At sixteen they would leave and try to find work or attend the local college four miles away. They would walk each day as very few could afford the bus fare.
- Each Lower School class had their own teacher but in the Upper School the teachers swapped round to teach specialised subjects.
- There was one computer in the school. This was kept in the head teacher's office to keep it safe. Unfortunately it didn't work yet as it had only arrived a few weeks before. The children had no access to the internet.
- There was no school uniform.
- There were no school dinners.
- There was no running water. At lunchtime a bowl was filled up in the entrance hall for the children to wash their hands.

Once satisfied that she had enough information Jenny thanked the teacher, who directed them to a bench at the front to watch the rest of the maths lesson.

It was strange to watch a lesson being taught to children in a foreign language. Jenny could see all their faces: some looked interested, others bored; some looked as if they understood the work easily, whilst others were screwing up their foreheads into puzzled expressions, trying to make some sense of what was being said.

The teacher moved her hands quickly, counting on her fingers, talking incessantly and drawing numbers in the air.

Jenny nudged Helena, "Why doesn't she just write on the blackboard?" she whispered.

"They've run out of chalk," Helena whispered back. "It ran out months ago and they don't know when they'll get anymore."

It was David's turn to ask a question now.

"Why is it that only four people are writing anything down?" he asked. "Aren't the others going to get into trouble?"

Jenny had become so engrossed watching the teacher that she hadn't noticed what the children were doing. Looking round she saw that David was right. Four children were scribbling numbers in their notebooks, the rest, including Ivonia and Stefan, were sitting in empty places trying hard to work out the sums in their heads.

"Things are very different in these village schools than they are in the main towns," Helena answered softly. "In this school children must bring their own books and pencils to work with. If they do not have them then they cannot write!"

"So you mean Ivonia and Stefan and the others just sit in every lesson and never do anything but listen?" Jenny was horrified.

Helena nodded again. "Many families in this village are too poor to provide their children with paper and pens. It is hard enough to feed them and buy them clothes."

"But Helena," even David looked stunned, "how can they learn anything?"

Helena shrugged her shoulders. "They just do their best. The problem is that if they don't do well at school they cannot get a job. Many of these children will leave here at 16; they will get married young, have children of their own and continue in a circle of poverty that they cannot get out of. Their children will be poor, receive a poor education, leave school with nothing, get married young, and have children and so on and so on!"

Jenny and David were silent for the rest of the lesson. It had come as a sudden, sharp shock to them that poverty stretched across every part of the villagers' lives. During the last two weeks they had come to accept that these people lived in rundown houses, ate meagre amounts of food and worked all the daylight hours to simply survive. But school, surely school should be different. They thought of their own classrooms where piles of paper lay in the recycling box, where you thought nothing of throwing away half used pencils and where you wrote in a different exercise book for each subject, usually finding that they were still half empty at the end of the year!

In that moment something changed in Jenny's heart. Suddenly she saw herself and all she had in a different light. No longer was she the unfortunate child whose dad had changed jobs meaning that all the extravagances she was used to had gone; instead she was a child who, in the eyes of children all over the world, was rich beyond their imaginations.

It was then that she knew she must try to do something to help. A plan was already forming in her mind. A plan that she couldn't carry out alone. What if ...? she tried to stifle the thought … What if Amy and I could do it together …?

A shiver of excitement and fear ran through her body. Amy was so good at organising things and it would be such fun to do it together!

A cloud drifted across the plan Jenny was making. It wouldn't be long now before they would return to England and she would have to stand face to face with Amy and make her apology. Jenny sighed. It would be so much easier if she knew whether or not Amy would be willing to forgive.

17 A sad goodbye

It was Sunday again and Ivan was due any minute. The week had flown by in a blur of walks, igloo building, snowball fights and serving warm refreshments alongside bars of chocolate at the potato field.

Despite the hectic schedule Jenny had managed to find some time alone when the children were in school and everyone else was busy working—she had so much to think about! Their time in Romania was coming to an end and Jenny was more and more aware that it was only a few days now before she would see Amy again. The idea that had sprung into her mind during the visit to school had grown into a full-scale plan. The more she thought about it the more excited she became. Now, as they waited for Ivan to arrive, she decided to confide in Mum.

"It sounds like a super idea," Mum said, obviously impressed. "But it will be a lot of work. You would certainly need some help."

Jenny looked down at the ground feeling embarrassed. She spoke softly. "I'm going to ask Amy," she whispered, avoiding looking Mum directly in the eye.

Mum said nothing for a moment. Jenny had been so much happier during the last few days. She didn't want to change that but neither did she want to build her hopes up too high.

"You know Jenny, Amy may not want to help," she said gently. "Try not to think about it too much or get too excited until you've talked to her."

Jenny nodded reluctantly. She didn't want to leave Ivonia and the other friends she had made here but at the same time she desperately wanted to get home to see Amy and find out if she actually could put things right.

Work at the field had recommenced in the middle of the week, as the worst of the snow began to thaw. Dad was disappointed that the project was not as far on as he had hoped, but he was happy to leave Ivan in charge until he returned in a few months' time. Jenny and David spent every unoccupied moment begging to be allowed to return with him—but for now, Dad was making no promises.

A farewell buffet had been planned for after church. Everyone in the village was invited to Ivan and Helena's and members of the church congregation were making food.

David was relieved it was a buffet!

"I can't wait to choose my own grub!" he announced gleefully. "No noodle soup, no soggy rice, no pig's ears, no eyeballs, no..."

"David! Stop it!" said Mum looking amused. "It hasn't been all that bad. We haven't had eyeballs once!"

David pulled a face. They had eaten almost every evening meal in the home of a different neighbour. Sitting round large family dining tables they had been served with a wide variety of unusual dishes. The children had struggled with many of the strange tastes and textures and Mum and Dad were very proud of their attempts to be polite and eat what was placed before them.

Each evening, on their return to the apartment, Mum
had disappeared into the kitchen and returned with a
plate full of goodies for each of them! Nothing particularly
special: a piece of bread, a slice of cheese, a few Pringles, a
piece of fruit, half a Mars bar and three jelly babies—most
of them brought from England—but it had become a treat
to look forward to when faced with some interesting meals
during the day!

"Do you remember Dad's face that night when Mum
said we couldn't have our midnight feast?" David asked,
starting to giggle. "I thought he was going to cry!"

Everyone laughed.

On Tuesday evening they had arrived home
particularly late, and as the electricity was still off, Mum
had announced that they would climb straight into bed.
Jenny and David had let out an agonized groan, but it was
Dad's cry of, "Oh no! Please, please, please not without the
midnight feast!" that had filled the room, making Jenny
and David cry with laughter, and making Mum scurry
into the kitchen, light candles and return with plates piled
high!

After that night every feast had been eaten by
candlelight, even though the electricity had been fixed.
The warm glow and the flickering flames dancing and
reflecting off every surface made the atmosphere homely
and beautiful.

"Can we carry on having nights like that when we get
home?" Jenny asked suddenly.

Mum and Dad nodded, glancing at each other, aware
that they were each thinking the same thing—how strange
that it should take a journey to a place like this to make

you appreciate the simple things in life. How many of
their luxurious holidays in the past could ever have taught
them so much or pulled them so much closer together as a
family?

*   *   *

The church service was, to the children's relief, slightly
shorter than the previous week! Three men had been
invited to speak, the second one was Andrei.

He smiled down at Jenny as he climbed into the pulpit,
making Jenny wonder if Ivan had told him about their
conversation in the potato field.

"Today my friends," Helena translated, "I will talk to
you about the Prodigal Son."

Jenny had heard that story many times before but this
time it was different. She had always thought that the
younger son, who wasted his father's money, was rather
stupid and that when he eventually came home his Dad
should have given him a severe telling off! Today, as she
listened, she found she understood.

The father was just like God, and we are like the
younger son. In the same way as the father forgave his son
in the story, so God wants to forgive us and welcome us
into his family.

"So the father ran to the son!" Andrei bellowed. "He
threw his arms around him and said, 'Welcome home my
precious son!'"

Jenny found herself smiling broadly round at Ivan. She
hadn't known those words were in the Bible! When she got

home she would find them in her Bible and highlight them to always remind her of the time she spent here.

*　　*　　*

Almost the whole village turned out to the farewell lunch. Old Mama sat presiding over the proceedings. She was the eldest person in the village. Jenny and David had visited her a few times at her tiny home with just two rooms. She lived, ate and slept in one room; they had never seen the other. Her long settee took up most of one wall with the brown tiled heater built in an L-shape round an adjacent corner. This was roughly the height of David's head with the stove in the bend and the hob on top of it.

Old Mama had shocked them on their first visit. Without warning she had jumped to her feet exclaiming in a booming voice, "Ask them Helena. Ask them, where they think this old lady sleeps in the winter?"

Helena had translated the question and both Jenny and David pointed in unison to the settee on which they were sitting. Without warning Old Mama had dragged them vigorously to their feet! Leaping into the air, she clambered like a monkey on to the top of the heater, pulling a blanket over her as a cover. Her body heaved up and down as she laughed hysterically at the amazement on their surprised faces!

Jenny laughed now as she looked across the courtyard to see Old Mama leap from her chair and clip a young boy round his head as he tried to cram another cake into his already bursting pockets!

She turned her attention to another group of men noisily gossiping near the house. Pavel, the smart village doctor; Adrien, whose wife was seriously ill but they could not afford any treatment; the men who had worked hard in the potato field, most of them with large families and no jobs; Andrei and Ivan with their hidden secret. She would miss them all when she left tomorrow.

Her thoughts were interrupted by Stefan waving a cricket bat dangerously near her head.

"Come and play!" he shouted delightedly in English, beckoning to anyone nearby.

The snow had gone now apart from small mounds marking the spots where giant snowmen had once stood or in shaded areas where the heat of the sun hadn't quite filtered through. It was a glorious day. The sun shone brightly and a gentle breeze blew, making the air fresh and clean.

"I think spring has arrived at last!" Ivan announced, fastening back the double gates so the spectators could watch the game more easily.

Most of the villagers joined in the match. There were no teams; everyone fielded unless it was their turn to bat. Any huge hit was met with an almighty cheer and a whole army of fielders fled after the ball, pushing each other playfully out-of-the-way, in a mad race to be the first to reach it. It was following one of these chases that Ivonia and Jenny caught a knowing glance from each other, detached themselves from the rest of the group and wandered up the lane to the potato field. They walked across the ditch—now complete with drain and rubble and ready to allow access to the land—and sat down on the tree trunk that had become their special place. They chatted and laughed and then fell into a comfortable silence, simply glad to be together watching the shadows lengthen as the sun sank in the sky.

"This is probably the last time it will be just the two of us," Ivonia said softly, each sensing that it was time to go. "We have had fun in this field."

"I know," said Jenny smiling. "The digging, the café, the snow ..." she paused. "... forgiveness."

Ivonia squeezed her hand.

"Forgiveness makes a friendship even more precious," she said smiling. "And you Jenny will always be my friend. I will never forget you."

"I will never forget you either," Jenny murmured. "You have taught me so much."

"And you will remember when you get home to your lovely house and other friends ... you will remember what is really important in life."

Jenny nodded, aware of a lump forming in her throat.

"You will remember ..." Ivonia continued, "that to have the love of God in your heart and to have family and friends around you can make you happy even if you have nothing else."

"I will remember," said Jenny. "And anyway hopefully I can convince Dad to bring me back here in a few months and you can remind me yourself!"

Both girls laughed.

"I hope you come back soon," said Ivonia. "And I hope you sort things out with Amy. I will pray you do."

The sun was beginning to set as they turned and began to walk back down the road. The view of the village before them was to stick in Jenny's memory for many years to come. The sky was layered in stripes of red and pink and a warm, rosy glow seemed to enfold the village with comfort and safety.

For a moment it was so easy to forget the poverty within the walls of many of the houses, and then a thought struck Jenny. In her mind she saw a picture in which the glow of warmth and comfort no longer came from the sun and the sky but from within each of the homes spread before her. A glow that shone brightly from each home where beautiful Romanian families had welcomed them, fed them and cared for them. A glow coming from people who selflessly gave from empty pockets and from hearts full of love.

18 Amy

The train was due any moment and Jenny was feeling a strange sensation of sadness and excitement. They had said goodbye to most of their friends the previous day; only Ivan, Helena and Ivonia had made the extremely squashed journey to the railway station.

Jenny reached into her pocket, gently pulling Ivonia a short distance from the group so no one could see what she was doing. She had told Mum her intentions and Mum had in turn told Helena so there would be no misunderstanding this time!

She held her clasped hand towards Ivonia.

"This is for you," she said. "I want you to have it ... to wear it ... and to remember our fun together."

She opened her palm.

"Jenny! I can't have that!" Ivonia gasped. "You love that locket! You can't give it to me!"

"I can!" Jenny spoke with certainty. "I can and I have! It's yours now."

She fastened it round Ivonia's neck. "When I get home I'll get two tiny photographs developed, one of you and one of me, and I'll send them to you so you can put them inside. Then I'll save up and buy another locket and put the same photographs in it. Then, even if we are miles apart, we can remember each other!"

Ivonia wiped her eyes.

"Thank you," she whispered. "I too want to give you a gift to remember ... it is nothing like yours ..."

She pulled a small wrapped parcel from her pocket and handed it to Jenny, who undid it carefully. Inside was the Romanian picture Bible that they had looked at on their first evening together.

"I can't take this!" Jenny exclaimed.

Ivonia held up a hand to silence her.

"You can and you will!" she said with such ferocity that all the adults turned and laughed.

"Doesn't sound like she will take 'no' for an answer!" shouted Ivan as the train appeared along the track.

"I will treasure it forever," whispered Jenny taking the book.

"It is a story that goes across any language," added Ivonia. "Goodbye my friend."

They loaded their luggage, hugged each person in turn and climbed aboard. The engines powered and the train began to move slowly away.

Jenny and David leaned out of the window.

"Byeeeeeee!" they shouted. "See you when Dad brings us back!"

They waved until Ivan, Helena and Ivonia were nothing but tiny dots in the distance and then flopped back into their seats.

"If Dad brings you back!" Dad reminded them, pulling a face.

"WHEN!" they both shouted together!

*   *   *

The delicious smell hit them at the front door.

Granddad had collected them from the airport and Grandma had a meal ready and waiting for them.

"Real food!" David sang at the top of his voice giving Grandma a cuddle. "I knew I loved you for some reason!"

Grandma pretended to punch him. David dodged out of her way.

"I thought you'd be ready for some English food," she laughed. "From the texts you sent me I thought you'd have wasted away and probably disappeared!"

"I have!" David replied, sucking in his cheeks and stomach to make himself look extra thin. "I'm like a lamp post!"

Grandma laughed and turned to Jenny. "You, my dear, look healthier than I've seen you in ages. Colour in your cheeks. Even a twinkle in your eye. The trip, I think, has done you good!"

It was lovely to sit eating familiar food, chatting non-stop about their experiences. It was as David crammed his third piece of toffee pavlova into his mouth and declared himself 'full to bursting' that Mum stood up.

"I know we've only just arrived home," she announced, "but Jenny and I have to pop out for a few minutes. We won't be long - just long enough to give David time to wash up! Come on Jen."

Jenny followed her gratefully to the car—she was in no doubt as to where they were going.

"You nervous?" Mum asked as Jenny slammed the car door.

"Very!" answered Jenny. "But thanks for taking me round so quickly."

"It's best to get things like this out of the way. You just be yourself. Say sorry and don't worry if Amy won't listen. You do your bit; the rest is up to her!"

They drew into Amy's driveway and stopped outside the front door. Jenny jumped out in a flash.

She hesitated as her quivering hand reached for the bell. She glanced back at Mum, who nodded her encouragement, and forced herself to press the button.

Brriinngg!

She heard the click of the inner porch door and saw a blurred image of Amy's mum through the frosted glass panel.

The front door opened.

"Jenny! I didn't expect it to be you!" Amy's mum seemed flustered.

Jenny drew a deep breath. "Is Amy in please?" she asked, aware that her voice had turned into a high-pitched squeak.

"Amy!" bellowed her mum.

Amy's feet were heard bounding downstairs and she appeared slightly out of breath.

"Jenny?" she panted.

"Please can I talk to you inside?"

"Okay!" Amy looked surprised. "Shall we go up to my room?"

Jenny followed her upstairs and sank down on the bed. She hadn't really had time to practice what she was going to say with Mum whisking her here so soon after they'd arrived home.

She opened her mouth, shut it and opened it again.

"Amy ... I'm sorry!" she said simply. She wanted to say so much more but somehow the muddle of words inside her head seemed unable to join into a complete sentence.

She waited silently for some response, her eyes lowered and her heart beating rapidly.

No response came.

Eventually she lifted her head to find Amy, her face wet, swallowing rapidly and trying hard to speak.

"It's not you," she sobbed suddenly. "It's not you ... it's me ..."

Jenny looked confused. "What do you mean?" she asked.

"It's me ..." Amy's words continued to tumble out. "I've been so jealous of you ... I thought you'd realised that day you were at my house and that you would never want to be my friend again! You were right! I was trying to make you impressed by my great big house and everything I had but only because I was so jealous of you ... you have so much more than I'll ever have!"

"Me ... more than you ...?" Jenny spluttered. "Amy you've got everything in the world!" Even in her wildest dreams this was totally unexpected!

Amy paused for a moment. "Jenny, you've got a Mum and a Dad ... I miss mine so much ... My grandparents have all died ... I will probably never have a brother or sister. You were always talking about the things you did at weekends with David and your family ... I don't have anyone apart from Mum ... and I was so ... so jealous... everything I had ever wanted ... it seemed you had it all ..."

Amy's voice trailed off as Jenny tried to take it all in.

"I'm sorry!" Amy whispered quietly. "I know you may not want to speak to me again now you know what I'm like."

Jenny could contain herself no longer. She burst into a mixture of hysterical crying and laughing at the same time!

"But Amy!" she began, fighting for words. "It was me that was jealous of you! I had no idea that you felt like that! I was totally jealous of this house, this bedroom and when you said you were getting a swimming pool ... well, I just snapped ... I'm so sorry!"

"I wanted to talk to you before you went to Romania," Amy continued, determined to get everything off her chest at once. "The only thing was I couldn't make myself because I was so jealous of that too!"

"Jealous of that?!" Jenny questioned. "Believe me Amy, we weren't staying in posh hotels like you'll be used to!"

"Exactly," said Amy. "I'd love to go off on an adventure like that, but Mum wouldn't let me. I know it's just because she wants to protect me... she's lost all the rest of her family... but I would so love to go somewhere different or dangerous or something!"

Jenny took hold of Amy's hands. Her eyes were shining but this time with excitement rather than tears!

"Oh Amy!" her words burst out in eagerness. "Let me tell you my plan. I had this idea in Romania and it's just got even better!"

It was half an hour later, when the two Mums had finished their coffee, that they decided to head upstairs to check the reconciliation had gone okay.

They found Jenny and Amy sitting cross legged on the floor surrounded by pieces of paper covered in hurriedly written lists. It was obvious from the girls streaked faces that they had been crying; it was equally obvious that the past was now forgotten and that they had moved on to new things!

"We need to go love," said Mum smiling. "I think David has had plenty of time to wash up! Follow me downstairs in a minute."

Jenny stood up, shaking the pins and needles out of her leg.

"I'll get my mum to talk to your mum!" she said quietly to Amy. "That will probably work better than us doing it. Then we'll make all the plans together. Oh Amy, I can't wait ... It will be even better with you there!"

19 A plan fulfilled

It had been a long tedious journey but at last they were approaching the Romanian border and anticipation was beginning to overtake boredom.

"I reckon four hours and we'll be there," Dad announced from the driver's seat. "Probably make it in three if we get through the check point quickly and go on ahead."

Jenny shivered, an excited tingle running down the length of her body.

This was her plan; her idea. Now it was actually happening!

Mum had been right, it had been hard work. One thing was certain—they couldn't have managed without Amy and her mum. It was a shame that Amy's mum had to work and so couldn't make the trip with them ...but Amy was here and that was what really mattered!

Jenny smiled at her friend sitting beside her looking eagerly one way and then the other, afraid to miss any little detail of the biggest adventure of her life so far. It hadn't been too difficult to convince Amy's mum that she should be allowed to come with them. Somehow it just wouldn't have been right if Amy hadn't been there. She had done so much of the organisation, planning and collecting and now ... a sign on the roadside announced their arrival in Romania.

"We've done it!" shouted David, making everyone jump. "We're here!"

The children turned round and gave the thumbs up sign to the driver in the small container lorry behind them as he too drove over the border.

Inside, the lorry was piled high with a massive collection of rucksacks of all shapes, colours and sizes. Each one was crammed full of school equipment. Jenny's idea to ask people to buy a rucksack and fill it with essential things for Romanian children to use in school had proved very popular. Together they had printed lists of ideas as to what to place in the bags; notebooks, pens, pencils, rubbers, rulers, chalk, calculators and of course sweets!

Jenny had given the talk she had prepared in a number of local schools and churches and even on local radio. Soon it seemed as if the whole town had wanted to help. The response was incredible. They had collected far more than expected—probably enough for each village child to have two or three bags each!

It was impossible to send such large quantities of material by post so Dad's charity had arranged for a lorry to transport the rucksacks, and without too much persuasion, Dad had agreed that he would drive in front of the lorry taking the family and Amy with him. And now they were almost there!

How different this was to her first visit to this beautiful country. This time Amy was beside her happy and smiling and very soon she would introduce her to Ivonia and they would have two whole weeks together. Added to that, it was the summer holidays and since there was no school,

Ivan and Helena had promised to take the girls along with David and Stefan for a few days camping up in the mountains!

Jenny settled back into her seat and gently fingered the new locket round her neck. She had written regularly to Ivonia telling her how the rucksack plan was progressing so that she and Helena could make the necessary arrangements in the village. There was to be a special ceremony in school tomorrow morning when each child would receive their gift. Jenny could imagine their faces shining and happy. It was such a simple idea but she knew it would make a big difference in the lives of children who had so little.

She remembered again Ivan's words following her first visit to Ivonia's home.

"They have nothing and yet they would say they had everything."

She hadn't understood then, but she understood so well now! Money and possessions can never make you truly happy; but love and forgiveness can fill your life with a wonder and a richness that overflows to those around you and changes the lives of people that it touches on the way.

DISCOVERING THE HIDDEN LAMB

Gill Jacobs

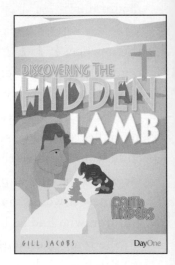

A story of two lambs: the orphaned lamb Ben cares for, and Jesus, the Lamb of God. Bible events woven into this story are seen through Ben's eyes as he struggles to understand who Jesus is while trying to save his pet lamb from being sold for sacrifice at Passover. The reader discovers what life was like in Palestine during Jesus' time, and why the Lamb of God had to die.

Much of Gill Jacobs' working life has been with young people both within the church and as a Paediatric Occupational Therapist. She runs training in special needs for professionals and has also been involved in writing parenting courses. Her husband John is a Messianic Jew. They live in Hampshire and have two grown-up daughters.

Also available

S.O.S. TITANIC

Jill Silverthorne

Chrissie and Luke Barwell are surprised to find themselves invited on a trip to America by an aunt they scarcely know. Their journey promises more than they expect when they secure a passage on the White Star Line's newest ocean-going liner. Chrissie, though, is uncertain from the beginning about what the trip may hold.

Based on events of April 1912, the journey turns out to be much more significant than any of the travellers could imagine. How will they cope with the life and death situations they face?

Jill Silverthorne was born and bred in South Wales and it was there she committed her life to Christ. She graduated from the University of Leicester with a degree in English and went on to teach at a sixth form college, before leading a faculty and then becoming deputy headteacher in a secondary school in the Midlands. Jill has always loved working with young people in her job and in church settings. She enjoys preparing youth-based resources for holiday clubs, camps and church youth groups. She has been published in association with her work and also worked with several Christian organisations, writing resources for ministries to teenagers. Jill has a passion to see high quality Christian literature written for young people in the twenty first century. This is her first contribution towards seeing that aim fulfilled.

Also available

THE SECRET OF THE HIDDEN TUNNEL

Mary Weeks Millard

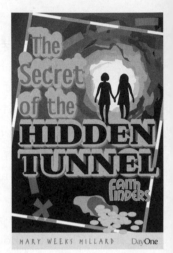

Matty Morris's world collapses when her parents announce that they are going to move to Africa and that she will need to go to boarding school. She is sure she won't like St Anne's, but she quickly settles in and makes friends. Through a series of adventures and personal challenges she and her friends make exciting discoveries about the school's history as well as some life-changing decisions ...

Mary Weeks Millard used to work as a missionary in Africa. She now loves to write stories for younger readers.

Also available

THE MYSTERY OF THE DESERTED HOUSE

Mary Weeks Millard

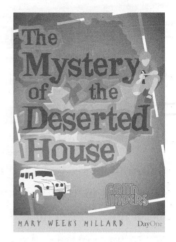

Spike, Joe and Matt are playing their usual ballgame when they find the deserted house. The gate is rusty, the grass is overgrown, there is a half-built extension, and an old Land Rover is abandoned in the garden. The boys are intrigued and, over time, start to explore the rooms inside. But the more time they spend there, the more mysterious they find it, and their exploration of the house eventually leads them into danger. What is the secret of this mystery house, and why did its owners leave it like this?

Mary Weeks Millard used to work as a missionary in Africa. She now loves to write stories for younger readers.

Also available

NEVER GIVE UP ON YOUR DREAMS

Mary Weeks Millard

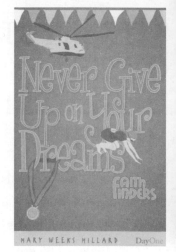

Gabrielle is six years old when her swimming instructor realizes that she has a natural talent and arranges for her to have extra swimming coaching. Through her dedication and self-discipline, and with the support of her family and especially her granny, Gabrielle gets better and better, and everyone thinks that she will soon be able to compete in the Olympics. She dreams of winning an Olympic gold. But one day, disaster strikes. What will happen to her Olympic dreams now?

Mary Weeks Millard used to work as a missionary in Africa. She now loves to write stories for younger readers.